And
I Still Fall For You!

Chitra Nandola

And

I Still Fall For You!

BY

Chitra Nandola

Originally published in India

ISBN: 978-93-89540-70-3 (Paperback)
978-93-89540-71-0 (eBook)

Published by RIGI PUBLICATION

777, Street no.9, Krishna Nagar
Khanna-141401 (Punjab), India
Website: www.rigipublication.com
Email: info@rigipublication.com
Phone: +91-9357710014, +91-9465468291

ACKNOWLEDGEMENT

I would like to first of all thank my parents and all the family members who supported me and have faith in me.

I would also like to thank my friends and two of my faculties Mr.Javed Nathani and Dr. Bhumika Achhnani who were standing as a support system for me and have faith in my work.

I thank my maternal grandfather whose legacy I've taken over. I would also like to thank my grandma who was constantly caring about how I'm doing and informing how much she loves me.

At last but not least I would like to thank all my readers. I love you all.

AUTHOR'S INTRODUCTION

I'm Chitra Nandola. I'm 21 years old and a growing seed in this beautiful world of writing. I'm pursuing an Integrated MBA with CFP and CAIM. I'm a blogger and a quote writer. For me writing is an art that confesses what is in your mind. Being from a Joint family I've this tendency to share things with my parents, my siblings, cousins everyone when I need something or I want to express something. So, I'm an open book sort of person but writing makes me alive and mesmerized!

Thank you so much even for your love and support for reading this book. If you want to share something about this book or about your life then I'll be available at the following platforms. I'm also including my bloggers ID, if you like my write up, do connect there with me and spread love!

Blogspot ID: itra.loveblogger
Instagram: itra.0510
YourQuote: Chitra Nandola
Pinterest: Itra

Regards
Chitra Nandola

INDEX

1. Did he just proposed me?   7

2. Rifting can be hilarious but what if the relationship is Just a month older?   18

3. Class Get-Together!   23

4. A new beginning!   30

5. Suddenly I lost the world!   34

6. He came to pick me up!   39

7. Love Letters rolled over in 21st Century!   48

8. He Complained, you don't meet me every day!   55

9. The way we wait for each other every day…!   61

10. Three Days!   67

11. Birthday!   77

12. Difficulties ruin our lives and lead us departed!   89

13. And I loved you for a thousand years!   103

A Warm Note!   105

"A time that faded over months but can never vanish from within me…

A Memory which is still alive in me and for me!"

I dedicate my first book to my late grandfather, my parents, family and my friends.

1

<u>Did He Just Proposed Me?</u>

It was the time when I left my home for my college studies. Like every person has their own dreams, I was also on my path for my new journey towards accomplishment of my dreams. It's going to be truly adventurous.

Being a varied personality, I've a number of things that I want to accomplish or achieve before I die. I shall be determined for each and every dream of mine. Like an advertisement of dairy milk says, "How far will you go for your love?" I want to work on each and every aspect of my dreams so that it completes with perfection.

It was my first night in this hostel and I was not at all able to sleep. I was scared of what will happen at college? How will my classmates and seniors be? What if they started ragging me? What if they tease me for what I'm? What if they laugh at me? What'll they talk about me when they see me for the first time?
What if I don't get good friends there? What if I acquire their bad habits? I was missing my mom-dad.

"I want to meet you. Where are you both, this place is not good. Please take me with you. I cannot live here. I cannot sleep here", my silent cries and tears were unstoppable. It was now difficult for me to breathe too.

I messaged one of my brothers (Crying). I told him, "I'm missing mumma, I need mumma, I don't know! I'm not feeling good. Things are scaring me. I'm afraid ...I...I..."

"Calm down dear, calm down. You are afraid because it's your first day there. Everything will be fine, don't worry and try to sleep while listening to some good songs… Okay? If u still doesn't feel good then call me. I'm there with you and please, don't cry. Crying is not the solution to any problems. We've to fight with it, right? And we can do that, right?" *He explained.*

"Hmm okay, bhaiya, I will try to sleep and not to cry. Thank you so much."

"Anytime sista! Good night and try to sleep? Take care of yourself and message me if you need someone to talk. I'm here."

"Okay, bhaiya…"

"See you!"

"See you!"

That night was truly horrifying. I wish I could have my maa that day with me.

Next day, I woke up around 5:30 Am and got ready for college. Everything was so jumbled, I've to take my bathing soap, detergent, washing brush, tooth brush, tooth paste, shampoo, conditioner, towel, clothes, etc. etc. I was so confused that every time I entered the bathroom, I remember to take something and come back forgetting another.

I was ready by 7 am but my college was at 9.

I called maa, and narrated all the things that happened. She was laughing at me. After a long conversation she sent me for breakfast.

Hell bad breakfast. The WORST I've ever had! Yukkk!

There was a one hour orientation program at our college. Everything was going well. I enjoyed the day at college. I was surprised to know that my class has only 13 students in it.

Never mind!

In this way days were passing with more enthusiasm, energy, excitement, happiness etc…

One day, I was sitting beside my hostel room's window. Weather was very glorifying and the sun was up brighter and shinier than any other day. I had a normal day, but a very tragic evening. Wind was passing through my hairs softly, kissing my face leaving the ascent of its existence. That adorable weather was calming my mind and providing peace, with earphones in my ears and listening to my favorite music. I was living that evening so gracefully and beautifully.

Some songs are so perfectly made for people like me who love the way it flows, music composed, how it is sung, depth of that voice and instruments that are playing notes. Every note expresses feelings, words, emotions and tries to make you feel that song.

Every feeling was soothing me. It was truly a blessed evening. Me in my white pajamas and light blue chicken kurta, a black bindi on my face with my hairs open. I was sitting with my pink teddy bear which had big eyes and a cute nose, surrounding my arms around it.
I made him sit on my lap, hugging it firmly, resting my head on its head and observing the movements of weather outside the window with a cup of tea in my hand.

(A Message popped)
He: Hey hii!
Me: Hello!
He: What's up? How are you?
Me: All good! But getting bored!
(He after a short conversation)
He: Hey can you give me a kiss like you are giving your sister in that picture?

Me: What? Are you serious? Are you screwed? We are friends, Okay!!! Friends do not kiss like that!!!

He: Calm down…calm down…calm down…!

It's just a kiss on my cheek. Nothing else. We are friends and we will be friends. Don't worry. Will you, please?

Me: No ways!!! *(Blushing)* I don't want to and I'll not.

(An Awkward silence)

Me: Bye. I need to go, I've submissions tomorrow!

He: Okay bye!

After some days he texted me again…

He: Hey! It's raining here.

Me: Wow! I wish it rains here too. I want to dance in the rain.

He: I wish I could send it to you.

Me: Yeah! Please send it here.

In a couple of minutes,

Me: Hey, it's raining, matlab how? What? What is happening? How can something come to you too soon when you wish to have it!

He: I sent you my love wrapping into the droplets of water. I wish I could watch you being crazy when this rain falls on you.

Me: Oooooo…Flirting hannn…

Hmm, ok now let me go to the terrace of the hostel.

He: Bye, Enjoy! Miss me…

And I went to the terrace. It rained extensively. I stayed there until our hostel guards didn't come to throw us out of the terrace. It was such a pleasure to be in the rain to feel the divine pleasure.

Rainy season is the best of all seasons! It makes me feel so loved, it makes me lost in deep thoughts about human relationships, about something which went wrong with me or if something is about to happen. And, it happened! I was thinking about Madhu that day, obviously not that I should accept his proposal of kissing him on his cheek or his statement that "I wish I can watch you being crazy when the rain drops falls on you"; instead I was thinking why he wanted that. Isn't it crazy?

And what if I fall in love with someone or someone builds a crush on me or if someone falls in love with me? Am I adorable? Will someone even like me? What if I become a joke for everyone? What if people start hating me? What if they don't even talk to me? What if I'll not be a part of any squad? My mood goes from good to bad in no time. This is the *benefit* of being an over thinker! And I appreciate that because there is no other way we can get rid of this!

During the vacation time, in the month of September, I was coming back to my hometown!

I was going home, for the first time from the hostel, after 33 days or more. Everyone at home was eager to see me after so long for the first time.

The moment I sat in the bus, dad called me.

"Hey, bus started?"

"Yep dad! It has. And I'm coming home. Yeyyy!"

"Yes, we are waiting. Come soon!"

"Yes dad, see you…"

"See you…"

I reached home after three and a half hours of long and not so peaceful journey. Dad was waiting for me at the station. He was very delighted to see me after so many days.

Papa, Mumma, my sisters, grandma and other family members, everyone hugged me. Mumma had prepared my favorite food for dinner. *That love is truly infinite!*

Did I forget to introduce myself?

Hey! I'm Parthvi… Namaste! And that message was from Madhu!
Madhu, one of my classmates. He is sinless, impeccable and one of the most handsome boys of our class. Haayyyeeeee!

So, I came to my town for my vacations and we were still good-friends, in fact more than good and we started chatting every day.
Madhu: Welcome to our town!
Me: Thank you mister!
Madhu: Soooo, excited to meet everyone?
Me: Yep of course. I can't wait to see my whole family. To see you all too.
Madhu: And, are you excited to meet me. (A Flirty Tone)?
Me: Yes…!!!(Blushing) But are you flirting on me?
Madhu: Ha ha! Do you think so?
Me: Yes of course! I mean, I can hear that tone Madhu!
Madhu: Yes! I'm and I was.
Can't wait to see you soon!
Me: Okay! We will make some plan of catching up somewhere. Our whole class!

Five months ago, in the beginning of the month of april…

I was chatting with him. It was our after-board vacation. It was the usual time of night when I chat with my group and a message popped in my inbox.

Madhu: Hey! I want to tell you something.
Me: Something to me! What?
Madhu: Ummm, I don't know how'll you react but
Me: But what Madhu?
Madhu: I… I love you!

                                                        Chitra Nandola

Two minutes of complete silence…

What the hell is going on? Someone just proposed me. What? I mean, Madhu proposed me. How…Why?

What did he see in me? Is this proposal for me? Did he really propose me……!!!!!!

I'm a girl with moderate brown skin and not so good looking. So being proposed by someone was a very shocking and big thing for me. That too by a handsome boy with a good physic and damn deep eyes.

Is he just flirting with me or is he teasing me? Is he playing with me? What if he is seriously in love with me? Will I weigh up to his expectation? And millions of questions rambled into my mind.

A message blinked on my screen.

Madhu: You there?
Madhu: You okay?
Madhu: Hey, answer me!
Me: Yep I'm okay, I'm okay!
Madhu: So?

Me Offline… I didn't give any answer that time. I was absolutely shocked and my thoughts were unreachable.

Next day, morning!
Madhu: Hey good morning…
But I didn't reply.

At noon, I met Heer. She came upstairs in my room.

Heer: Hey.
Me: Hii.
Heer: Did something happen?
Me: Yes, I guess!

　　　　　　　　　　　　　　　　　　　　Chitra Nandola

I showed my chats to her and to verify if he is not cheating me, she called him to meet us at Varanasi ghat-3 at six in the evening.

I explained her all my feelings and problems while she consoled me. We were eagerly waiting for D-Day.

Actually, for me this time was an *"Imtehaan ki ghadi"*. Things for me were tougher than it might appear. My mind was continuously evaluating the things and time felt like it had come to a standstill.

I cannot even think of what was going to happen but I was curious and nervous too. One side there were dreams, the other side fear of breaking the same. One side my heart was jumping from excitement other side my mind was rolling imaginations of me coming back to home with broken heart pieces in my hands.

My heart, brain, hands, legs were shivering with fear, excitement and skepticism.

Let us see what will happen now.

6 o'clock in the evening,

I and Heer reached before him and waited for him to come. Madhu arrived there along with Vickey.

Vickey was one of my classmates from high school.

Heer asked Madhu, "Are you telling the truth? Are you seriously in love with her?"

(My heart by the time was like dhak dhak---dhak dhak)

And he replied what felt literally very rude and insulting to me.

He said (Laughing): No-no-no-no. Sorry, I was just kidding and I didn't tell her this. It was nothing like that and I just wanted to know how she reacts. Love with this girl?!!! No ways dude. (Continuously laughing)

Heer: You sure? You were just kidding? I've all your chats. You can't lie to me.

He: No-No. There is nothing like that. I was genuinely kidding.

Heer held my hand, pulled me towards the parking and we went back to our homes.

A mere sad and horrifying night for me. Not because he didn't love me, but because he played with my emotions.

I cried not because I thought I was ugly and no one can love me. I cried because he altered his words and insulted me in-front of Vickey and Heer.

Heartbreak hurts but insults hit the worst. He was continuously laughing at me, holding his stomach with both his hands. His laughter was rigorous as my heart was being grated every time I saw him laughing or hear his laughter.

After a couple of days. A message blinked.!

Madhu: Hey!! I'm sorry about that day but I didn't want to confess it in-front of Vickey and Heer. Then our whole class will mock us. Please don't mind.

Me: I'm really sorry. I cannot believe any of your statements. It's, It's very difficult for me to trust you or your statements, Sorry.

Madhu: Sorry yaar but I love you. I love you a lot!

Me: See Madhu, Actually, I don't have that sort of feelings for you. I've never felt that thing for you. See it's, It's out of my syllabus. If I don't feel for you, how can I accept this proposal? Sorry Madhu, please try to understand.

Me: Sorry.

Madhu: So, we are no more old friends now?

Me: Yes, we can be friends.

Madhu: Thank you!

Me: Never Mind.

So, back to that day when I came back home for my vacations! After a few days it was the end of the month of August but without much rain or cold. That fine day I was shivering. I was not in a good state of mind. I was at my dad's office. That was the first time ever I

realized that I've started liking him. In-fact I've fallen in love with him.

Why I did and how I fell for him is something I thought I would never describe. All these months he has not skipped a single chance of influencing me. From caring for me to worrying about me. From asking me about "How was your day?" to fixing a bug occurred on that day. From commenting romantically on my pictures to making a folder of my pictures. Everything he did has flaunted me to make me fall for him, to miss him, to make me curious about him and to make me '*FALL FOR HIM*'!

I immediately messaged Heer.

Me: Hey, Something has happened to me. I'm in a miserable condition. I am really confused.

She: Tell me what has happened. What are you feeling? What is in your mind?

Me: I think I'm in love. I think he made me fall for him. I want to meet him Heer, Do something, Please do something.

She: You sure na?

Me: I don't know. I'm afraid.

She: If you are sure then we can fix a time and catch up with Madhu sometime today and you can talk with him.

Me: Yes, Please make it happen.

She: Ok then. Calm down. Message him that you want to meet him and call him at our place.

Me: Okay.

I dropped a message and told him that I wanted to meet him and we will meet at 7.

I, Heer and Madhu met there beside a boat so that no one could recognize us there.

For a few minutes we all were sitting in complete silence.

Heer: Madhu. Parthvi wants to tell you something.
Madhu: What do you want to tell me?
Me: (*Smiling, nervous and in a pin drop silence*)
Heer: Parthvi, say what you want to tell to Madhu.
Me: Nothing. What? Ummm
Heer: If you both want to stay quiet then I'm leaving.

Me: no-no-no-no wait! wait!
Ummm okay.
Madhu! I wanted to tell you that.
Madhu: Tell me what?
Heer: Wait Madhu, let her complete.
Me: Yeah so I was saying that, that I Love you!
(Finally, I said it. Wow! What will he react! Shiii! Isn't it awkward like after 4.5 months I accepted his proposal)
Madhu: (Blushing + Shocked + I don't know what else) He smiled and said, "I love you too!'

~

"BESHAQ BADE PYAAR SE MILE TO HAI HUME VO...
KYA SAATH BHI REH PAYENGE SAARI UMRA VO?"
-ITRA

2

<u>Rifting can be hilarious but what if the relationship is just a month older?</u>

Yeah! It is exactly what you are thinking. Break up in a month! How? What happened? How did it happen? Blah! Blah! Blah! Like every coin has its two sides. My Madhu also had his own two sides.

Like falling in love with an ugly girl by a handsome hot boy is very rare. And I thought it happened to me. Isn't it strange! That's basic, right? Every handsome guy and beautiful girl does that. He was not unique.

No doubt it is wrong but it's a mindset. My guy loves skinny girls with straight hair. But that wasn't the personality I carry. I was not attractive that any guy can like me in just one look. But at the same time one more question arose, why did he proposed me then? If he wants to cheat on me and he doesn't love me then why did he propose me? Yes, those questions arrived in my mind too! It was a completely unbelievable and shocking thing for me that someone played with my feelings even when I chose not to, the time when I was being proposed.

Anyways, no one can stop the evitable. Its life and it is its nature. And I respect that, though being so rude.

So, what happened was, one day after coming from college I called him. We were talking and sharing secrets with each other. It was like me sharing more and him sharing less of the secrets. So, I asked him, like every boy in our class did you also like Madeline?

Madeline is one of the most beautiful girl in the whole school. Skinny, beautiful, intelligent, stunning, with sweet tantrums and everything a boy would ever seek in his girl.

He said, "Yes."
I asked, "So, still would you like to go to her ? Do you wanna still be her man?"
He said, "Yep, maybe if I get a chance to do so!."
I replied, "Ok, then you can go and ask her if she likes you or not. I won't mind. We can still be friends."
He asked, "Are you sure you will be fine if I leave you for Madeline?"
I said,"Yup. It's ok."

And he said "bye" and went away.
I cried a lot and a lot. I cursed myself for being so ugly. I cried like hell a lot and was unable to breathe.
Half an hour passed away, Vedika returned from college and came to my room.

Vedika, my best friend who made me strong and even spoiled me a lot. A person whom I'll always admire for my entire life.

She saw me and asked me what happened. For a few minutes I didn't say anything. I was catching my breaths. She hugged me tight, wiped my tears, gave me water to drink and asked me to calm down.
Then she asked again, "Teddy tell me what happened."
I showed her my chat.

Man! She reacted. Bloody rascal he is. How the hell can he use you? And how the hell can you answer him like this and then start crying so loud? I'm very disappointed. Let me talk with him.

She didn't talked with him being Vedika. She messaged him and talked with him on behalf of me. So that he thinks it's me who is talking and not any third person.

She took my phone and messaged him 'hii'
He replied: hey.
I told Vedika to swear that she wouldn't use any bad words no matter what.
(Of course I will stop her as I was loyal to him! My feelings were real and his were reel!)
She replied: I need to talk.
He: Yeah sure. What happened?
She: If you loved Madeline then why did you propose me?
He: But.
She: But what hann? Am I a use and throw pen? What do you think of yourself?
He: But she will not agree on my proposal.
She: Ooo! Wow! So, you proposed me because she will not accept your proposal? Do you have a mind? Are you hearing yourself?
He: Ok tell me what should I do then?
She: What do you mean by what should you do? Don't you have any sense?
He: I'm sorry yaar.
She: In the beginning only, I told you that I cannot break your trust. If I don't have that feeling for you, I cannot accept your proposal, still you did this to me!
She: How dare you dude? How dare you man! Don't you ever try to call me or message me. Do whatever you want to !
He: Sorry! Do forgive me if you can.
She: Bye!
He: Bye.
And we broke up!

Wasn't I right that day? Who am I to stop him from going to whom he loves and wants to be with? And after all, it is a rule of the world that outer beauty is always admired by the people.

So, something unforeseen and unanticipated happened.!

He proposed to her and she rejected his proposal as she was already engaged to a boy of her caste, which was not known by Madhu. But I knew that. So what happened after that is, she blocked him from everywhere and called me. She told me everything they talked about. I told her what happened since he proposed me till that day. We discussed the matter. She explained to me that I should've understood this before he proposed to me, that he can betray me but I didn't. Our call lasted for 45minutes and at last we were smiling and laughed at what had happened.

After the call ended, I blocked him from every application and my phone too but he existed in my mind, brain, heart and memories. And then fucking I cried again and again and again every day.! Every day I blamed myself for falling for him. I also tried to console myself but I failed every time. Vedika and Heer, were by my side. Still I cried! Afterall "I had to bear the fruits of my own actions"

Past then, he tried to reach me many times but I didn't respond as it was 6th of October, just two days before my birthday he did this to me. It was very, you know I mean; when u broke up two days before your birthday. So I was very sad and disappointed that day and even my birthday went worse! No doubt I got so many phone calls, wishes, messages, statuses, Insta stories everything But without a single good friend attendee. It was okay, the day passed by and everything was over.

I'll love to mention one thing here from that day. A day before that I received a parcel from my mom. So I went to the courier office to get that parcel. On my way to the hostel, I was very excited to see what my parents and siblings had sent me for my birthday.

I opened the bag, It was full of things like chocolates, Cadburys, a cake, soya sticks, dress for my birthday which was orange colored, netted one piece with white pearl and golden jhumka earrings.

I wore the same dress with a half pony with a side puff and whitish golden heels.I went out for the whole day, ate Maggi, pizzas, cold drinks, pastries etc. On that day evening, it was probably the best part of that day. My dad sent a boy with a box of Kaju-katri. It is basically a sweet which I love the most which I shared with the hostel warden, my roommates and other friends. I slept early that day, missing his presence and tears filled in my eyes.

Everything was getting worse day-by-day. Crying, late night wake ups increased, weeping silently every time! It was totally unbearable and indigestible to me. I was in literal shock! No doubt it was just a month old relation but what hurt me more is my loyalty and the way he ditched me. The way he said that Madeline couldn't have said yes that's why I proposed you. The way he was not affected, the way he left me two days before my birthday, the way he tried to use me, the way he threw me after he got what he wanted. Everything was deep inside my mind. Everything was ruining my mind. Everything was destroying my brain. I felt like the most unluckiest person on this earth. Disgusting! Pathetic! Unfair! He was a disgrace in the name of love! And by the way what he did, it was not love! And you know what it was… it was just shit!

~

"BADA LAJAVAB ANDAZZ THA UNKA JAANE KA…

RULA KE BHI GAYE AUR VAPAS AANE KI UMEED BHI DE GAYE!"

-ITRA

3

<u>Class Get-Together!</u>

A class get-together! Wasn't it a bad idea for our toxic relationship? Who guesses what will happen but everything happens for a reason. Let us see what destiny has planned for this get-together! Hope it does not make things complicated!

On the 8th of November, we all met at a ganga ghat. Except 2-3 people, every one of us were present. Me, Rahul, Madhu, Krishna, Madeline, Easha, Hardik, Varin, and Vinay.

First, I, Krishna, Varin and Madhu reached. We greeted each other, shook hands and I hugged Krishna as well. I was talking much with Krishna and Varin and not with Madhu. I was ignoring his presence.

Krishna is one of my best friends. With whom I used to talk at the time of my troubles and of course when I'm happy or any emotion. He and Heer along with Vedika were there with me. Yeah but he didn't knew about me and Madhu being in a relationship as I was afraid of telling him and being scolded by him.

So, on that day later till the time everyone had arrived four of us took selfies and talked about the college life of ours.

And then one after the other Rahul, Madeline, Easha, Hardik everyone arrived. Everyone was very happy seeing all together after months! All started teasing, hitting and roasting each other. Then we played hide and seek.

After some time, we took photographs and went to eat something as hunger was killing us. Everyone convinced me to pay as a treat as this will be considered as my birthday treat. But I didn't carried much cash with me. We ate Chinese, Dry Manchurian, gravy Manchurian, Manchurian noodles, triple fried rice followed by cold drinks. With every increase of order I skipped a heartbeat remembering the bucks I've carried. But Krishna knew this thing from the beginning. Krishna came to me at the time of paying and we splitted the bill. After having everything we went to Momo's shop to have Vinay's birthday party whose birthday was on 16th October along with Madeline. Then we went to Madeline's dad's office. We met her mom, dad, aunt and aunt's baby boy. We played with him and Madeline's mom-dad bought ice-cream for all of us. Her mom clicked pictures of all of us.

It was already 9 o'clock in the evening and we decided to disperse. I told Krishna to drop me but he told me to go with Madhu as he was going by that side. I didn't wanted to go with him. So, I told them to let me go by walking. My aunts' home is near and I've to go there as my family is there. No one agreed with me and sent me with Madhu.

I sat behind him on his bike. I didn't even hold him instead I chose to hold the stand which was on the back side of the bike.

I was in a big hornet's nest! I was in a big dilemma or paradox you can say. It was like my brain was in a big can of worms. I was unable to think of what I should do and what I shouldn't!

Madhu: hey.
Me: ..
Madhu: I'm sorry.
Me: ..
He put a break on his bike. Due to the sudden deceleration, I came forward losing my control and leaned on him. It was visibly intentional. It happened exactly as he thought of but I went back so that I wouldn't get lost in my feelings for him. No doubt they were not lost, just kept

hidden deep inside me. But he did the same for a couple of times again and in the last one time I held him from the back of his waist. Holding him again was a damnnn. I got lost again in that feeling. And he stopped the bike near my aunts' street and we greeted each other and he left.

But, his presence in me didn't. I was blushing again. The minute I climbed the stairs, Heer saw me blushing and confused! She understood that something had happened there. First, everyone started screaming at me and asked me where I was till now? What took me so long to reach home? All were staring at me horrifyingly.

After that when everything settled, Heer came to me. and started staring at me. Her eyes were asking me what had happened there? So, I asked her "What?" She replied, "What?" I didn't know what to reply so I asked her again, "What? Nothing has happened, don't stare at me like this! Ok! I'll tell you later sometime."

I messaged Krishna, "Why did you do that? I didn't wanted to go with Madhu. I could've walked. No need to worry or else you come to drop me!"

Krishna: But it was very dark. I couldn't have left you walking alone and what issue do you have with Madhu? Huh?

"Nothing Krishna, I just didn't want to go with him. I don't like him, that's it. Try to understand."

He: I read both of your eyes clearly that something wrong has happened. But I want to talk to you later about the topic. And can you please tell me what you have been hiding from me since days?

"Krishna it's nothing. Seriously. Trust me. There is nothing like that.

He: Do you swear on me?

"Ummmm! Please Krishna. Okay I'll tell you later my battery is about to die. Even I'm not home yet. I'll message you after reaching home."

                                    Chitra Nandola

He: Okay! Do message me otherwise, I'll hit you hard. If you don't then I won't talk to you for the rest of my life. I cannot see you like this. If there is any problem, we will solve it together. Message me fast.

"Hmm! Okay Krishna. Tata. See you."

He: tata!

Later on that day, I went back home with my parents and siblings. My mom-dad again scolded me for coming late at aunts' home.

Finally, after reaching my room, I messaged Krishna and Heer. I was simultaneously talking with both of them.

First, I messaged Heer and told her everything that had happened there! She said, "It's okay and we should tell everything to Krishna now. Otherwise it will be a huge disaster for us."

So, I made a What's app group of three of us.
I messaged Krishna, "Come into that chat room. I want to confess something."
Krishna: Hey!
Me: Hey!
Heer: Hey!
Say it Parthvi!
Krishna: Yep! What happened?
Me: Ummm! Krishna.
Krishna: What?
Heer: Speak Parthvi!
It's okay. Tell us!
Krishna: Bolona be *(Say it na)*!
Me: Ummm! Krishna… I and Madhu were in a relationship!
Krishna: What?
When?
Why didn't you told me this before?
What were you waiting for?

And...and were matlab? Aren't you now?

Me: Ummm! Krishna I'm sorry.

Let me explain.

Krishna: What? What sorry huh?

Okay explain!

"See Krishna! What happened is.

When he first conveyed his feelings to me. I was very shocked! Later he also declared it as a prank. I and Heer went to meet him. He said he was just playing prank. He said sorry. Afterwards he told me that he seriously had feelings for me."

Krishna: Then?

So, I told him that I don't feel the same for you, so I cannot cheat you or play with your feelings and emotions by accepting your proposal."

Krishna: Then?

"Then, about four and a half months later. I had fallen for him...and..."

Krishna: And?

And when I came back from vacation, I messaged Heer about this and we went to meet him. Then, I proposed him and received "I love you too" in return.

Krishna: And you didn't even bother to tell me. Right!

"Arree...no no we were about to tell you but everything went wrong. It's nothing right now. We just broke up in a month...! And that's it..."

Krishna: How did you break up...like what he did? Did he use you? Did he cheat on you?

"No... Maybe yes. I don't know..."

Krishna: Tell me exactly what happened?

"Okay, wait..."

I explained everything to him in detail.

Krishna: What the fu#k? How dare he? Let me talk with him. I'll screw him up!

I and Heer remained quiet till the time he added Madhu into the group. He was trying to make Madhu confess.

Then he started to ask me questions too. Which madhu had already answered.

Ultimately, we set foot on an unbelievable end. I and Madhu need to understand each other before coming into any sort of relationship. "Madhu what you did was wrong! Don't you ever do that again and I'm again asking you… Do you still love Parthvi? Tell me what exactly you feel… No force or pressure on you but I cannot see her crying."

Madhu: Yes Krishna! I still do. I'm sorry for what happened, please forgive me.

Krishna: Hmm…both of you be happy! Love u both…

Me: Love you too Krishna.

Krishna messaged me personally.

Krishna: You happy?

Me: Yup... But confused too!

He: It's ok! Take some time and if you feel that it's not going right, then come to me. Okay? Give him and yourself some time to settle.

Me: Yep! Hope so! lets see…

He: Okay now it's your turn, you have to do a favour for me.

Me: What?

He: I love Heer. I want to confess my feelings to her and it can be possible only if you help me to do that.

Me: Woahhhh! Okay, so are you prepared? Have you composed what you want to tell and how will you?

He: Yeah but I'm nervous!

Me: Okay wait!

(New Group Created:- Me, Heer and Krishna)

Me: Hey!

Heer: New group?

Me: Yep, for a beautiful purpose.

Heer: What?

Me: Someone wants to confess something to you!

Heer: Who? Krishna?

Heer: (hann! Krishna bolona!) Yes Krishna! What do you want to confess?

Krishna: Ummm!

Me: Yes Krishna! Speak!

Krishna: Will you be my girlfriend?

(Heer messaged Krishna in personal)

Heer: What answer should I give?

I mean I don't know what to say and how to say!

Krishna: Just say, "Yes! Like our friendship! Always and forever"

Heer: Okay!

(Heer messaged in the group)

Yes!

Me: Woahhhh! She said yes Krishna!

Krishna: Hmm! Like our friendship! Always and forever!

Heer: Yep…*(Blushing!)*

Me: Oo shit! Madhu is messaging me!

What will I talk with him now? How will he start a conversation? Like how will I reply to him?

Heer: Chill! Chill! Everything will be fine. Reply to him. He must be waiting.

Krishna: Yup! Don't worry. Reply to him. In case you need us, message in this group.

Me: Okay… and you both enjoy!*(wink)*

By the way, congratulations Janemans!

Krishna: Thank you*(blushing)* and you too*(winking)*

Heer: Yep!*(Laughing)* thank you and all the best to you too!

Me: Arghhh! Those naughty expressions of you two! See you.

Both: Babye…See you.

~

"DUR HONE ME BHI ALAG HI KHUDGARZI THI…
PASS AAYE TO SHUKAR RAB NE BHI LIKH DIYA!"
- ITRA

4

<u>A New Beginning!</u>

A New Beginning! Isn't it strange and something which is abnormal! Like after something ends like this! Now it was somewhat out of my comfort zone. I was not as much open to him as I was before. I was not getting much connected towards him in the fear of losing 'ME' once again! I cannot see myself like what I had become! It was totally unrealistic for me.

Madhu: Hey! You there? Can we talk?
Me: Hey! Yup! Sure.
Madhu: I'm sorry for what I did.

*Wait wait wait… Before we proceed forward, let me tell you something, I saw Madhu today, when I passed by his dad's shop. He looked damn stunning and my heart was like dhak dhak dhak dhak. Black tees, dark shining eyes, his beard and moustache, that flaunting hairs. Oo shit! He saw me staring at him and our eyes met but I ignored him and left quickly before he got to know that…**THAT… I STILL FALL FOR HIM! EVERYTIME I SEE HIM!***
Okay back to story…back to story! It's not time to lost in him right now!

So, he said sorry for what he did and he didn't wanted to hurt me and apologized for everything!

I said, "It's okay, but I liked what you did. You confessed the truth to me. I'm happy about that. In this way if any such thing happens then do tell me whatever the truth is. Don't you ever hide it."

He: Okay…I promise! Thank you!

Me: My pleasure !

He: Parthvi!

Me: Hann Madhu!

He: Parthvii! I love you...

Me: Hmm…love you too.

He: Shall we meet tomorrow at our place?

Me: Let's see. Even Heer and Krishna were planning to meet. We'll meet together somewhere.

He: But…

But we will not get our time then…

Me: Are baba! Don't worry. We will. Trust me!

He: Okay! I trust you.

And the chat goes on till both of us fall asleep with phones on our hands.

~

"Good morning…"

"Good morning madhu…"

"So we are meeting today, right?

"Amm… Yeah but I'll message you in a while at what time we are meeting… Okay?"

"Yep! For sure. Will wait for that moment to see you again."

"Hey!" *(I messaged in our group of me, Krishna and Heer)*

Krishna: Hey!

She. Hey!

Me: Good morning guys!

Krishna: Good morning darling.

Heer: Good morning people.

Me: So what are the plans for today's hangouts? When are we meeting ?

Krishna: Anytime is feasible for me.

Heer: Let's meet sharp at 5:30pm?

Me: Okay done! I'll come to pick up you, be ready at 5:20.

Heer: Okay done.*(Thumbs up)*

Krishna: Okay done!

Me: Yep. Then see you there.

Both: Yep…babye..
Me: Babye.

~

Me to Madhu: We are meeting sharp at 5:30pm, behind kings palace! Do reach on time. Don't be late and pick up calls.
He replied, Wowww! Okay done! I'll take care of it. Thank you so much. Love you …
Me : Love you more!

~

At 5:35pm.
Me and Heer sitting over there waiting for both of the boys. Heer called Krishna, he told her that he is on his way. I called Madhu but he didn't received it. I called him once again, still he didn't received it.
Krishna arrived with chocolates, chips and cold drinks…

We hugged each other and I told Krishna to call him once again. He did, but as usual,"The number you are trying to reach is currently busy. Please try again later." That sweet voice of disappointment.

"It's ok Krishna, he must be sleeping or stuck somewhere."
Three of us were talking, laughing and drinking but I was waiting for him. My eyes were searching for his mere presence.

It was 6pm! *I saw him coming towards us, white tees that white face with a hefty beard look!*

Hayyyeee! He came near us and greeted Krishna first then to Heer, so I was watching him with my hands folded. I wanted to act like I was angry with him, but his innocent smile and handsome face melted my heart.
Madhu: Hey…
Me: Hii!
"Where were you? Why so late?" All of us started questioning him.

Madhu: I woke up late and then papa called me at his shop for some work so I was stuck!

Krishna: At least you should have received my call if not her because of your dad.

Madhu: Sorry sorry!

We continued eating chips and cold drinks.

We shared our chocolates bite by bite. Initially I denied to show that I was angry but he didn't listen and forcefully gave the first bite to me.

Krishna: I and Heer want some personal time. We want to go for a walk. We'll be back soon.

Me and Madhu: Okay! No issues. See you.

(They both left)

Meanwhile Madhu held my hand and we saw each other.

You know what, an eye contact with the person you love is more romantic than a kiss!

So, I turned myself and shifted my eyes to somewhere else. Like Oh My God! *Bass!* And we smiled…

He came close and kept his arm around my waist.

Now my right ear is right beside his long and damn hot neck. He pulled me near. Now I'm completely surrounded by his arms… Just me and him!

He planted a beautiful sign of his love on my cheeks and firmly intertwined his long skinny fingers with mine's . We barely spoke a word, we were just lost in the warmth within and the peace around.

~

NAZAR MEIN JO AA RAHA THA VO NAQSH BOHOT GEHRA THA…

LEKIN JO IS DIL ME THA VO BHI TO VAHIN BAHON MEIN GHERE BETHA THA!"

-ITRA

5

<u>Suddenly I lost the world!</u>

Some things are wonderful but some are fascinating! Some things are what you dreamt of and some things just flow on your way and you feel the 'WOW' factor about them!

One day we were normally talking. He demanded that kiss on cheek which I mentioned above in chapter one. Sometimes it's good and sometimes it isn't, that he remembers even the tiny little things and I've to even retain a small thing which I've to buy from somewhere. It happens! Sometimes I forget why I came to that place or forget what I was saying in just a second!

I said, "Okay, we are meeting today so will give you what you deserve today but just one."

He: Only one?

"Yesss! Only one."

He: This is unfair!

I told that *vahi purana vala dilouge: "Everything is fair in Love and War" and I laughed out loud...*

He: So rude!

Me: Ha ha ha ha!

"See you soon. Tata."

He: Tata! Love you more…

Me: But I don't*(Wink)*

~

I was waiting for him at the Ganga ghat.
And he was there. For the first time, he was on time.
We found a place where we can't be recognized.

We hugged! And he planted a kiss on my forehead. Warmest kiss ever! And we sat down!

He drew me to the same position; one arm surrounded from the back side of my waist and the other from the front, every inch of my right ear entirely touching his warm neck!

So, we were just observing the water, sky and the moon ,everything so peacefully. I was doing chattar-pattar chattar-pattar and he being a so-called **"GOOD LISTENER"**, *listening to every bit of it. Moreover he was watching me and my gestures and flaws and staring at me like you know with his "Katilana Nazar."*

He was continuously glancing at me and admiring the beauty, that made me a little shy and made me feel uneasy. I held his face tight with my tiny fingers and forced his face away from me. I couldn't hold his face long enough as he pulled my hands back and brought his face back to the initial position.

Then I just closed my eyes and leaned on him, So peaceful it was. He was softly skimming his one hand on my face while the other was still protecting me!

After this moment, everytime I met him, we would be always sitting in the same position and Everytime fall asleep in his arms. It felt tremendously gratifying and peaceful.

And this way we started meeting everyday. Same place with the same warmth and feeling of protection.

Everything was going lovely and delightful. We both were happier than before. My love for him increased exponentially by each passing day. I kept falling for him again daily as a new day showed me a better version of him. The way he smiles, the way he protects, the way he cares, the way he loves, the way he sees me, the way he walks, the way he talks, the way he adjusts his schedule just to talk with me, the way he is always ready to help me in my chaos! Like everything! Each and every atom of him! I felt him hugging tighter and tighter. He is cute but his endearing and enchanting gesticulation were cuter. I don't even have words to explain how he smiles through his nicely set moustache!

One fine day he asked for my permission.

"What permission?", I asked.

He asked me, "May I kiss you? Like a quick one, not the French one!

Me: What? Are you crazy? No you cannot! I mean why?

He: Please Please Please! I insist.

Me: Please don't force me. I don't like to get physical.

He: Please parthvi.

Me: No!

I messaged Heer: Hey, he is asking permission for a quick kiss! I mean yuk... Is it all necessary? I don't want to do that. I don't like all those things. please tell him not to force me.

Heer: Okay, don't worry. If you don't want to then you don't have to. I'll tell him not to ask you again, okay. Now don't worry. Krishna and I, We have made a plan and all four of us are meeting today.

Me: Okay.

I messaged Madhu: Four of us are meeting at 6pm at our place!

Madhu: Did you tell them about that permission?

Me: No I didn't. I just discussed it with Heer. She said she will tell you not to.

He: Damn!

Me: Obviously! I'm not comfortable with all these things. I'll not allow you to do that until I feel right about it. I inform you again, DON'T FORCE ME.

Madhu: Okay... I won't force you anymore. ·

Me: Hmm okay...

He: Okay see you... See you in evening!

Me: Okay! Bye..

~

Tiringggg! Tiringggg!

A message Popped on my phone.

'Dear students,

Your final examinations are beginning from 13th of December. Please prepare yourself for the examinations. Your hall tickets will be available soon. Do collect it from the admin office before 5th of December. All the best!

Regards

Principal'

Ooo! Shit! I've to reach college in two days. Now what? And the examination dates were near. I'm not yet prepared.

Me: Maa! Papa! I have to reach college within two days. I've to collect my hall ticket and my examination date has been declared. They are from 13th December.

Maa-Papa: Great! So start your preparations.

Papa: I'll book your tickets.

Maa: How will we manage everything in just a day?

Me: Maa don't worry. I'm going for only 15 days. Nothing much will be needed.

Maa: Then too we have to prepare something for you. It's okay, I'll do the rest of the things, you just start preparing and start packing your bag. Tell me what is needed and left to take… Okay?

Me: Ok maa…

~

These two days passed with hell lot of work and the last day I went to meet my love in the evening, to wave him bye before I leave.

We met, we hugged, and we shared the warmth. This time he transposed me on his lap facing him.He hugged me tightly and asked me not to leave. "I'll miss you." I held his face with my hands and said I'm coming back for my Christmas vacation in 15days. Okay…

He: Hmm…*(and hugged me tightly)*

My arms around his neck and his surrounding my waist. He took my both hands in his hands and pulled them towards my back. Held both of my wrists in his one hand and in a quick seconds till I understood what he was actually trying to do, he held my face and kissed…!
"Status: LOST!"

I was unable to sleep, I was mum, I drove home with a sense of breakup in my mind. In short I was totally blank and wondering in an unbelievable, implausible and in a far-fetched state of mind which I was not able to understand what just happened!

~

"JO SAPNO MEIN NAHI SOCHA THA SHAYAD VO AAJ HOGAYA…
JO WAQT KO AANE MEIN ABHI WAQT THA, VO PAL-DO-PAL MEIN HI AAGAYA!"
-ITRA

6

<u>He came to pick me up!</u>

Everything was going extraordinary well! Five months later, in the month of May he came to Siliguri, the place where I was studying! So, the plan was he would arrive there in the morning by 10:00am and wander around until I finish my last examination and then we would hang out together.

Actually, I'm a night person. I was reading at night for my last examination. I was blushing! Imagining! Concentrating back to book! Re-blushing! Again Imagining! Going back to book. I was imagining us holding each other's hand! He hugging me! We walking on footpaths! Sitting in the garden! Watching our first movie together! Holding hands! Tangled fingers! Eating together! Clicking pictures together! Meeting! Going on the same bus! Hayyyyeee! Imagining! Diverting mind! So happy! So enthusiastic! And whatnot! I read till 4:00am still couldn't help myself to sleep as I was still thinking about the time we are going to spend together!

Then he called me at 6, to wake me up. I answered his call in a sleepy voice.

He: Hey good morning (*Whispering*)

Me: Hmmm! (*Still sleepy*)

He: Hey wake up bachha!

Me: Good morning. Please let me sleep for some time. I slept after 4 o'clock.

He: Hmm okay. You can sleep. .I'll wake you up again at 7!

Me: Hmmm

Chitra Nandola

(**Tittttt** Call Hung-up)

I called him in the morning at 6:45 am to ask him if he has reached the bus stop or not!

He answered so enthusiastically, "Yes I have reached the bus stop. Yeah I'm coming, Can't wait to see you."

"Yep me too! Come soon… Acha okk call you later I need to study. I can't let my exam suffer.

So as usual one of my *"Jigri yaara"* from my college called me in the morning to ask me when I'll be ready. We have this tendency that every morning of the examination he will call me, come to pick me up and then we sit in a garden or outside the college where our examination center is and I'll teach him the important notes so that he can pass the examination.

(*Meet is calling*)

He: Good morning… You up?

Me: Good morning… Not exactly.

He: So when are we meeting?

Me: At 7:30 or 7:45. I'm very sleepy as I slept at 4. Please give me some time to get fresh.

He: Okay then, Wake up it's already 6:55…

Me: Okay I will…Tata

"Okay Tata" and He hung up.

I informed myself, "Okay sweetie now you have to wake up anyhow but still you can sleep for 10minutes. Good ninu."

Blanket on, eyes close and lights off!

Tringgggg Tringgggg   *--phone rang--*
Madhu is calling…

"Ooo god! No one will let me sleep!"
I woke up, got ready for exams and for Madhu..

I wore a dark red short kurta paired with blue jeans bended from the bottom. I applied kajal and eyeliner and kept my hair half open and flaunting, wore my college ID and skin colored heels.

Meet was already waiting there at the gate of my hostel.
I ran down stairs and climbed up his scooter as we were getting very late now for our final revisions.

~

Finally the paper is over. He must be waiting.
I Switched on my phone, saw 5 missed calls and 6-7 messages.
I called him and asked him where he was. Did he reach or not?
He: Hey! Where are you?
Me: Outside my college gate and you?
He: Find me if you can…...
"OMG are you kidding me? The sun is hot and it feels so damn harsh. Okay,let me try"
"Hahahhaha!"
"Don't laugh Madhu."
"Okay okay I'm not" (*Still in a laughing voice*)
"Hey you are behind that chole-puri wala, beside the mobile cover shop, right? Don't hide now. Come out! I found you. Okay let me cross the road and come over there."
I went there and he took out his handkerchief, wiped sweat from my face and hugged me. That 5'8'' long him and 5'0" me. I could barely reach his chest.

We got a cab, and I asked him to take us to Reliance Inox.
We took some selfies. He held my hand and came near me, pushing himself away from the edge. He keeps staring at me when I am gazing at the road and I serendipitously correspond the same.

Break!!! Cab stopped.
Behenji cinema aagaya, said the cab driver.

                                                              Chitra Nandola

"Okay bhaiya, how much.'
"50Rs"
"Lo…Thank you!"

~

"You downloaded the tickets?" He asked.
Download? (I asked him confusedly and in cute unaware voice)
"Amm…No I didn't know we had to do that!"
He pulled my cheeks and said, "Buddhuu after booking the tickets you have to download them too and show them to the security guards. Give me your phone,I will do that or else we'll miss our movie."
"Hmm okay, Take this."
"Password?"
"I've your finger print too in my phone's security. *(Wink)*
He saw me with a dangerous look on his eyes.
"Okay"
"Shall we leave?", I asked.
"Yep, let's go.", He said enthusiastically.

He made me walk forward and held my hand till the screen after the security check was done.
We entered the theatre, reached our seats then took a deep breath. I asked him for water. My bag was with him, he took out my bottle, opened its cap and passed it to me. *(Hayyyyeee…he was a dream come true type person. So damn caring and these little-little gestures of him, made me love him more every time)*

I asked him to have a sip, he took one. The part of the bottle where his lips touched while he was drinking was my target. My next sip was from that side.
I tried to recover from those cute lovely imaginations of ours, it was difficult to succeed.

It is a rule in India that before a movie starts, playing The National Anthem is compulsory.
We stood up for that proud moment, In complete position of 'Savdhan'.
"Jaya hai…..
Jaya hai….
Jaya hai…
Jaya.. Jaya.. Jaya.. Jaya hai…………." These lines of the anthem always gives me goosebumps.

After the anthem, I discovered that I was sitting on his right.
The movie started! "Bahubali-2 The conclusion." was very fantastic. The music, the action, the cinematography, everything. I was lost in the movie but he had already watched the movie. He liked the movie so much that he insisted on watching. He has an advantage there. Just because he has already watched it, his complete attention was on me. He was observing my reactions and expressions, the way I was coming forward and leaning back on my seat, the way I was getting emotional, excited and sad while watching the movie. He observed everything.

He tangled his left hand fingers into my right hand fingers, held it tightly and we both got back to the movie.
After sometime when I again leaned forward being excited about the scene but he pulled my hand to get me back. This time not only my palms but my whole hand until my shoulder was beside his. He and his fondling give the major couple goals.

Few moments later he pulled my elbow towards him so that I could put my head on his shoulder and watch the movie more comfortably. This time my whole hand was under his custody. Our elbows crossed and fingers still tangled. He firmly kissed my cheek. My eyes widened to tell him not to do, in a way trying to scare him. Again we tried to get back to the movie, Actually me, not him. He was watching me and not the movie.

I was watching him wholeheartedly but I've never found myself getting enough of him. That crave of mine is never gratified. NEVER! Not even today.

Let me take you to today's *Deedar Scene.*
I was going from that same road, he was sitting at the same place. He was playing a game on his phone. I watched him for more than 2 to 3 minutes. All my organs, mind, heart, eyes, that smile on my face, every muscle, every cell of my body got into a very different level of happiness. I cannot even explain how I felt. I must have died there only. He looked breathtakingly awesome! ***And I fell for him again!*** How could someone be sooooo much astonishingly awesome! Damn it!

"KYU YEH TUJHE DEKHNE KI CHAHATEIN PURI HOTI NAHI...
KYU BAAR-BAAR TUJHE DEKHNE KE BAAD BHI, TERE DEEDAR
KI YE PYAAS BUJTI NAHI...!"
-ITRA

So in the movie when Devsena and Bahubali's scene comes he tickles me. I'm very sensitive to tickling. I get vibrated in just a site full of wanting to tickle me!

And the ending fight comes. The sound and every kill in the movie scared me. I held him tightly. He was laughing at me and enjoying those moments. I mean how can someone be so mean with the person they love! In the end of the movie he pulled both my cheeks with a broad smile in his face.

I held his arm as I didn't want to go out. I wanted to be with him there!

Then we went out. It was so hot out there. We booked an Ola cab till the U.S. Pizza. We ordered unlimited meals for both of us and went to take our plates for salad.

We were eating from our plates and also sharing bites with each other. *(So in love naa! That cheesy thing...hahahha...but remember they hurt the most when the relationship digs!)*

Ooo my god Madhu it's fucking 5:30pm! We have to rush or else we will miss our bus. I called my known rickshaw uncle to pick us. We paid the bill for whatever few things we ate. We rushed towards the rickshaw. That uncle took us to my hostel to collect my bags and sign the leaving note of the hostel.

"Madhu, you wait here.", I told him at the corner of the hostel. He got out of the rickshaw and we proceeded towards the hostel. I already called my roommate to bring my bags to the ground floor. She was already there before I reached. I signed the note she helped me in putting bags in the rickshaw, hugged and waved me bye.

Madhu sat in the rickshaw and I told bhaiya to move as fast as possible as we have no time now.

When we reached there, the bus had already left!

We took another rickshaw till the circle to ask for another bus. Unfortunately there was no bus going to our hometown. Then we took one more rickshaw towards the last stop of the city from where we can get a local bus.

And we got one.

"150 bucks per person", the conductor exclaimed!

Ok so 300 for two, we paid him and got a seat near the driver's seat. It was not a seat, it was basically a passage where extra passengers can sit!

We both were tired and I was worried.

I called my dad, and informed him that I found a bus and the bus had departed. I will reach there by 10:30pm.

He said "Okay, take care."

I said ok and hung up!

He was observing other things and my eyes were totally stuck at him…!

I was observing his gestures, I was satisfying my thirst of seeing him, I was unable to keep my eyes somewhere else, my eyes wanted to see only him.

After nearly two hours have passed.

Conductor and Madhu sent me to an empty seat, so I went there. But the best thing about that seat was I could watch Madhu easily. He was right in front of my eyes, so lovely, so in love, so cute, so dashing, ahhhh and what not!

After like 20-25minutes passed, 25% of the bus got empty. There were 2 corner seats empty in the last row so we went to sit there.

I sat beside the window and he was on my left.

We slept, me on his shoulder and he kept his head on mine. So mesmerizing! One earphone in his ear, one in mine, love songs on! Wind! Travelling! Everything was perfect!

Now our town was about to come…so I called dad!

Dad bus has entered the city, come soon! So before dad came I told him to leave the bus quickly as our stops were the same! He waved me bye and left. The moment he left, dad arrived! I hugged him, took my bags and left for home.

I'm a very talkative girl so in the whole way home I was sharing things with my dad about the pizza, the movie and the examination. The only difference was I was not with Madhhu for him, I was with Vedika! *(Wink)*

And I reached home. Everyone welcomed me. I went for a bath as I was in the worst state! And after having a bath I hugged everyone and we had dinner as they all were waiting for me.

When I went to my room, I slept on my back and was staring at our ceiling imagining him and was smiling, blushing, and was recollecting today's events. That holding of his hand, that couldn't take my eyes from him, that leaning on him, that resting my head on his arms, that intertwined fingers, movie, lunch everything!

What do you think, I'll ever find anybody like him ever? Or will he stay with me forever?

~

Chitra Nandola

"BOHOT HI LAAJAVAAB SUKOON THA UNN BAHON MEIN...
NA KOI DARR THA, NA KOI FIKRA...
AUR KYA KHUBSURTI SE NAVAZI THI MENE MERI YE
MOHABBAT...
USE CHHAND SHABDON SE KHUSHI THI AUR MUJHE USKA
IZHAAR KARNE MEIN!
-ITRA

7

Love Letters rolled over in the 21st Century!

Being a 90's kid, I too love to express my feelings over letters and being in love with him made me more curious to exchange them. He is not that much of an expressive type and writing a letter for him was a very very difficult task.
I was his caption writer and He was my calendar!
I was his poet and he was my poetry.
I was his words and he was my shayri.
Total combination of an extrovert and introvert!
On 26th May 2018, I wrote my first letter for him. No doubt I've expressed my feelings through shayaris but still the magic what letters do is where I wanted to get lost!

To My Dear one,
Lots of Love!
Maybe I'm very annoying, maybe I overreact in my worst situation, maybe you hate my company sometimes but I'll make you feel so special for being mine. Yeah I'm immature, unbearable, an idiot, a cry baby, an over reactive, sometimes arrogant, rude etc, but I think you can handle my flows and love me more. Yeah I want you to be by my side forever, I want to hide in you, I want to hug you tightly when I'm saddest or happiest. Yeah I want to go for long drives with you, sitting behind you hugging and not wanting to utter a single word. I want to sit beside you and hold your hand when you are not okay. When happiness doesn't kiss you, I want to make you sleep on my lap and calm down and fall asleep.

With love
Antra

Miss you…

ANTRA! Basically he is a movie lover, so whenever he goes for any movie both of us get our new names because according to him, he is the hero and I'm the heroine of every movie.

He narrates the story of the movie he watched, I narrate the story of the novel I read!

To Ghelu,   *27/05/2018*

Love you so much…
Your Sparkling eyes! Your badi wali smile! Your natkhat vaali harkatein! Whenever I remember it makes my day. It's very difficult for me to come out of these thoughts after recalling them.
I don't know when we'll meet for hours but I want to hug you tight!
Okay whatever! I cannot do anything about this so let's not talk about this right now.
Acha sunn na, ek task kal ke liye?
Hann no doubt you have to wake up a little early for that but i think it's okay! I already know we have gained traits of kumbhkaran.
And by the way I missed you yesterday, because you slept early, then I saw the moon from my room's window and GAMEOVER! As you know he is my first love, don't get jealous okay.
Love you so much…

From
Chand ki Chandni
I'll tell you task on phone call(wink)

Like every love story is different in its own this is also a *Patakha* story for me. An introvert starts sharing everything with you, when that person

                                    Chitra Nandola

sings for you, cares for you, writes letters for you, dances with you, It really feels like winning an Oscar!

28ᵗʰ May 2018

I'm very sorry for sleeping early yesterday. I was very sleepy and unable to stop my eyes from getting shut.

By the way I want to tell you something. I want to meet you on a regular basis no doubt, but since a few days I'm not feeling like coming alone in the late evenings to meet you. It scares me.

It is of other people or of yours that I don't know but it really scares me a lot.

I want you to be with me at every step of my life but then why is this fear eating me? What makes me so scared of you?

Why does that confidence lack? Why I cannot rely on you in everything? What made me feel this?

With love

And definitely not less because of what I wrote, my love for you will be infinite forever.

Love you Haathi!

Sometimes it is hard for a girl to trust a guy at times when he meets her regularly in the evenings. No doubt he is my boy, still it was scaring me a lot and may be because I'm scared of nights. I don't know exactly but there was one more thing in it, I don't want to make physical relations beyond my limits. Maybe that scares me. He is a very nice guy. He can never cross my limits. He knows me, I would kill him if he did so!

29/05/2018

From Bindu

I was recalling memories at Heer's kitchen, when I was elected by our group for cooking maggi and that vessel was so high that I was unable to reach there.

I seriously want those moments for my entire life. I'm wearing a saree, you come and hug me from behind and tickles me.
Most favorite dream moments of mine!
I come out after bathing with my wet hairs and stand near the window to dry them up and you wake up and come near me and tease me in a little romantic manner.
But there is nothing to rush about, these all things can be done after we get married. It is not the right time now.

Okay, Love you
See you!
Tata

Its mind blowing, How we create our imagination with the person we love and to be with us for our entire life. Those lovely imaginations and those thoughts that blush every time is the result of your "Love is in the air!". Those little-little things will make your world go round!

30/05/2018
Hmm... Finally I'm coming today to meet you. So janab aapka intezar ab khatam hota hai. Ae-ae one minute one minute what if someone finds us hanging out together?
*   Madhu: You cannot do this hann! That's unfair! I've been waiting for you since days. Don't do this please please.*
Are calm down nothing will happen. Uncle has gone out of station so no chill.
Yeah by the way going for a two days holiday, if possible, for sure will come to see you before leaving!

With Love
Yours one and only!

When you come to your hometown and your love is also from your hometown then it's very hard to balance between your family and him. Like what time should be allotted to whom? If you give more attention to any of them then the second one will definitely eat you raw! Hahaha anyways, still things will go on and time never waits for anyone!

Next day, I was going to my maternal grandmother's house. I gave my today's letter to him with the previous one itself and told him not to open it before morning.

31/05/2018
Good Morning darling!
Ahahahahha... Today's letter in the morning itself. No waiting and no buffer hours or minutes! Lucky hann!
> *By the way no special note for today but yes check your whatsapp at 1:00pm...*
> With love (Wink)

Surprises excites na! me too! But even if I'm planning for someone else! It gives me immense pleasure when I see someone smiling because of me and of course why not something for him! Yeah by the way I sent him a recording, a song sung by me. And I still remember his expressions! Hayyyeee!
He was missing me a lot so he heard that song in loops! We can't talk on call but now he can hear me through the recording.

01/06/2018
Good Morning Seth!

So, what is special about today? Amm! Have to think of it!
Acha listen! I'm cooking today's lunch at home. Like one step towards my married life...hahahaha(Wink)

Okay listen, there is something below your ear, go and check yourself in front of the mirror...rush! Did you find anything?

 Chitra Nandola

Oo yeah right that's my lipstick's mark. Take care hann so that aunty couldn't find it and your engineer brother!
Okay now bye hann... Let me concentrate on cooking. Who knows if some magic happens? (Wink)

I mean leave romance, let me concentrate on cooking otherwise my mother-in-law will not let me come in.
Tataaa...

Love you...

Seems cool na! How we pretend some unknown person to be the love of your life, to be mother-in-law, my to be father-in-law, to be brother-in-law, that respect we give them that love emotions we share. Sometimes it's so strange that we admire and love them so unconditionally to whom we've never met before! That feeling is felt by everyone but understood and realized at different different times...

Let's see how many more colors this story shows!
So my last letter of this season was on 2nd July 2018. Last because then in few days my college was starting and the letter goes like this:

2nd July 2018
Aapki nazron ne samja pyaar ke kabil mujhe...
Dil ki ye dhadkan theherja milgayi manzil mujhe...
Aapki nazron ne samja...

I really really love your eyes. The way they shine, it's simplicity, it's beauty, that depth!

Eyes are the part that attracts the most to me. It catches my heart and attention first towards anyone. From my favorite list of them, yours are my favourite. I love to read them, feel them, catch it's attention towards me and alas! Meet them and never want to take away from my eyes!

                                    Chitra Nandola

And I still fall for you!

With Love
Bhodki...

My feelings for him can never fade, that depth of love, that bond, that chemistry people use to be jealous of us except Heer and Krishna. They are perfect.
It was like Ravindra Singh's book title: "Love that feels right!"

Disclaimer always comes before a movie starts but in my case I'm giving this in the end so that you don't kill me for what I'm going to share!

Disclaimer!
All the letters I added in this chapter were kept with one of our friends as one of my letters was found by his mother and she yelled at him! And the rest of the letters were given by him two or three in number. My maid threw them out at the time of house cleaning. She thought I'd kept my waste papers under my bed! And I'm really sorry for it! because I cannot even ask her where those papers are…!

But I loved the way he expressed his feelings too in these letters! As I told you he is not very expressive but that little effort of him made me ***Fall for him again!***

~

"KITNI SHIDDAT SE KI THI MENE USSE MOHABBAT…
NA KOI UMEED THI NA KOI SHART BAS MOHABBAT HI
MOHABBAT…
SHIKAYATEIN TO FIR BHI AAYI, KYUKI SHAYAD USKI
UMEEDON PE NAHI KAYAM THI MERI YE BESHART
MOHOBAT!"
-ITRA

8

He complained, you don't meet me every day!

"Please please please please Parthvi! Don't say 'no' today. You have to come to meet me. That's it! I'm not going to listen to any of your 'cannot come reasons'. You are coming! That's it!"
"Are baba! I can't! Please try to understand dude. Everyone is at home. I've to be here."

"But you know na, It's been 2 days since we haven't met!"

"Madhu, It's only 2 days. There are so many people at home today and I cannot take such risks! You know that if I can, then I would've surely come. Like every time I do."

"But what is the issue hann?"

"Are you insane? Do you have any idea what you are saying and what do you want me to do? Like seriously! You are not getting this thing in your mind?"

"Okay bye. I'm going there and will sit there till 9:30pm. If you can come and meet me then good otherwise don't. I'll be waiting for you…"

"But I can't man! And it's just 7 right now. What will you do there for 2.5 hours? Because I assure you that I will not be able to come and meet you!"

"Will see!"
"Please try to understand Madhu."
"I won't!"
"Okay then sit there till 9:30. I'm not coming."
"But still I'll wait.."

"Its okk keep waiting."
"Bye!"
"Bye!"

~

"This is his everyday and every time scene, Heer. You know sometimes it's very difficult for us to move out of the house especially when we have family gatherings and all, right?"
"And is it necessary to meet daily? I can't. I usually go and meet him but sometimes it's impossible for me to go!"

"He should understand this na?"

"Obviously he should and this type of persistence should never be fulfilled. It's your mistake that you managed every time to meet him whenever he did this type of demand. You shouldn't have earlier."

"Yeah I know, it is really a big mistake of mine. I shouldn't have done this earlier! What has been done, is done! What'll I do now, that's the question. He will get angry at me."

"If he gets angry then let him! You don't need to be sorry. He can't even understand that you are helpless?

"Hmm okay, let's see."
Heer! Parthvi! (*Mumma proclaimed*)
"Yes mumma!"
"Yes aunty!"
"Come, the dinner is ready. Everyone is waiting at the table."
"Okay, mumma!"
"Let's go…",said Heer "and don't stress much. It's fine. He needs to understand this thing no Matter how stubborn he is. Do explain him well otherwise I and Krishna will for sure make him understand."

"Yep okay, I'll try. "

~

"Hey!"
"Madhu!"
"Please reply."
"I'm sorry. Please please try to understand man…"
"What hann!"(he yelled)
"Ok do whatever you want I'm no more explaining anything. You think I'm wrong, then I'm wrong!"
"Yes, you don't even bother what's going on in my mind!"
"Yes, you are right."
"Acha madhu, I'm very sleepy. We'll talk tomorrow."
"Na! Talk with me I said!"
"I'm sleepy. Good night."
(Data off!)
Usually what we see that whatever your girl is saying is right! But here it was total vice-versa!

He says don't go out after 10:30pm! He calls me from his bathroom that did I reach my Pg or I'm still roaming around the city. He ensures that I don't take much time out after my classes end. He ensures that I don't go out with my boys squad much.

But it irritates me a lot. Like why you are screaming on me for everything. I'm not a small girl. You are possessive for me no doubt! You love me a lot I understand! But it's ruining my mind every time. It is my life I can think of what is right and what is not. What is the big deal? And there was not even any security issue but he didn't understand this thing.

One day, I was sitting with Vedika and Varun at the stairs in front of our pg's society and he was calling me continuously when the clock showed 10:30 to him. He was doing lots and lots of messages to me. Vedika and Varun also got angry when I was answering his calls. Varun said ,"Give me his number I'll handle him. Let me talk to him $#%^!h*&…"

"No no no Varun I'll handle. Calm down calm down!"

                                         Chitra Nandola

"Hello!"

"You are still out?"

"See Madhu, I don't like your all this so called pressure on me okay. I'm like a free bird. I cannot handle your insecurities and over possessiveness! Whatever is there, keep it with you. The more you will push me towards all these nonsense things the more I'll get far from you. I'll not bother to tell you when I'm going where and to meet whom! When my classes ended or when my college ended. It's enough of your restrictions"

He got angry and hung up my phone but in a few minutes, he messaged me again, "Have you reached?"

I was like, "$u%^! What the hell is this man!"

And three of us ignored the message and started singing along with the song, our favorite one(Wink)

"Bewafa Sanam tari bovv meherbani" It is a very famous song in gujrati. We enjoyed hearing that being non-Guajarati too. That feeling was at it's different level."

Everything every time ends with me crying or yelling or not talking or ending up doing what he wants. Most of the time the only last option works along with me crying and frustrating hell lot!

But it was obvious for him not to understand these things because after a bunch of explanations too he always stands in the same place from where I took him. So the displacement is always zero in this case, according to physics law!

~

So the next day in the morning I didn't message him after waking up.
Not even a Good Morning text!

His message came after 11 am.

"Not even a good morning text hann! So much angry on me hann?"

(I didn't replied)

"At least reply. I know you are awake."

(no reply)

"Areeyyy yaarrr! I've called you 10 times since you said bye at night and at least reply to those messages."

(still didn't reply)

(He calls me)

"Hey…!" I said

"Where are you? Why are you not replying to my messages…?"

"I don't know…"

"Acha tell me are you okay?"

"Yep! I'm alright."

"But you don't seem to be!"

"Nope! I'm good." *(with Little sobs)*

"Hey, are you crying?"

"No! I'm not. "*(sill sobbing)*

"Okay! I'm sorry. Please don't cry."

"Hmm…"

"Parthviiii please…"

"Hmm…"

"So are we meeting today? Please for 10minutes not more."

(kya insaaan hai be ye…abhi to kal ki baat ke liye mujhe sorry bolu and now he is offering to meet me today!)

"Will see…" , I said

"Okay, take your time and inform me soon."

"Hmm okay…"

"Bye."

"Bye."

~

(I called him)

"Hey I've left my home. Come soon I've only 10-15minutes with me."

"Okay okay I'm coming."

(*Call hung up*)

I reached there and he took more than 2 minutes to reach there.

And he was here!

We went beside the Ganga ghat together.

As usual he tried to hold my hand but I didn't allow him to. We reached at the end of that wall and he held me through my waist. I tried to get rid of that trap but I couldn't.

"Sorry Parthvi! *Please maaf kardena...* "

"Please na... You cannot do this to me."

"It is your every time issue. You don't want to understand my situation. I'll not bear this thing now.

(Then he bent down on his knees, held his ears and apologized)

"I'm sorry! Please forgive me please parthvi..."

Bass wahin hum pighal gaye (Wink)...

"It's okay. Next time, take care of this thing and try to understand things before forcing me for anything. It hurts me."

"Okay...", he said...

With so much excitement and delightness he hugged me, pulled my cheeks and kissed my left cheek and forehead.

I buried my head in his chest and surrounded my arms around him. For some time, for that peace that I was craving for!

He held my hand and we went back to parking as I was really in a hurry.

~

But still after his every imperfection he has damn perfections which every girl craves for! And I love all of them, each and every one of them till the date...!

"CHAHE LAKHH BURAIYAN HOGI USME...PAR USKI ANDER KI KHUBSURTI USKE PYAAR MEIN CHALAKTI THI... CHAHE LAKH BAAR MUJHE VO RULA DE...PAR MERI MUSKURAHAT HAMESHA USKE DIL ME KED THI..."

-ITRA

2

<u>The way we wait for each other every day…!</u>

Waiting for someone is tedious but waiting for each other seemed so enthusiastic and curious to us! It makes my heart skip a beat, the moment he calls me. My heart jumps out of nowhere! And that blush on my face, butterflies in my stomach. That widening and that shine of my eyes when they see his name blink on my phone screen!

From morning till night no matter how many times he calls or we talk, my heart always skips a beat when he calls!

He wakes up in the morning . He goes to his bathroom to call me and wake me up. That my hangover sleep, I don't drink but my morning struggles of waking up seems to be like that of a drunk person. He calls me to wake me up 2-3 times and if I won't wake up *fir to aafat hi aa jati hai.* And if it's 8:00am then it's over! How much cuteness you will show there will be no effect on him. Hahaha… But I used to enjoy that a lot. He wakes me up with the warmth and that vibe of love. It feels like a shield of love.

If I accidentally or by mistake wake up early at seven then I will plug in my earphones, play any of my favorite songs, sit on a swing with the toothbrush in hand for half an hour. Will groove on songs or will feel the depth. Depends on my mood. Till the time he doesn't call me I'll not even get ready for my college. Then if he takes a lot of time and my buffer time is over then and only then I'll rush for my work.

'He was like my morning tea.'

I couldn't have made it out for college or for birthday wishes if he would not have been with me. But anyways time flies and people take an exit from life when their time with us gets over.

Yeah by the way today also *"Tera deedar hua...pehla sa pyar hua...pehli hi baar hua iss dil ko"*... He was in Tomato red t-shirt talking with one of his employees. He looked the same way! That eyes, that beard, that moustache, that smile, that hair and that super glowing face. Hayyyyeeee!!! ***And I Still...***

So I was telling,

That beauty of morning when I woke up listening to him. You can obviously imagine the level of happiness and the level of feelings and emotions...!

After that, he will call me while he is on the way to college. Mostly at that time I'm about to leave for my college like almost ready types!

Oo god it's 12:30 he must be calling in half an hour...

Hey Parthvi wait...*(A voice came from behind)*

(Principal sir...gone!)

"Yes sir! "

"Come to my office I've some work."

"Okay sir."

"May I come in sir."

"Yes come in. You all have class for an hour at our theatre room, so don't go anywhere and call all your classmates and sit there."

"But sir..."

"No but Parthvi. Just do what I said."

"Okay sir. Thank you sir!"

"Ooo shittt! Now what?"

I ran towards my classmates, They were sitting in the open theatre of our college.

"What happened? Why are you running?"

"Principal is calling us for an extra lecture in 5 minutes at our theatre room on the 3rd floor." *(Out of breath)*

"Are baap re!"

"Lets bunk it and go somewhere else!"

"But it's principal sir!"

The moment I was trying to explain them they just held my hand and pulled me towards the parking lot. We took our vehicles out, ate chaat, sat in Prince's red car and drove towards the outskirts of the city. We stopped at a bakery, ate muffins and hung out there.

(*"Mukhtasar Mulaqat hai...ankahi koi baat hai"* my phone rang)

Madhu Calling!

Heyyyyy...(I greeted in excitement)

"Hey! You seem to be very happy! What happened?"

"Hahahah..."(I Laughed)

(Explained everything to him)

"So, Lucky hann! Okay so reach home early before 2:00 otherwise you know me."

"Okay baba. Bye."

"Okk bye. Love you..."

"Hmm you too..."

(Phone hung up....)

I hate this thing, I mean restrictions of timing. It's ok let it be. You enjoy it. Forget it. (Explained to myself)

~

This was the time when I used to wait for him to call. Most of the time I fall asleep till the time he calls me after leaving college. He loves to hear me when I'm asleep, that voice of mine gives him immense pleasure.

There were days when he used to video call me at night and we used to talk in sign languages. Then he makes me sleep by patting his hand softly on my head. Obviously from the phone. That sweet gesture. It has become our routine now. He makes me fall asleep watching him and after some time he'll hang the call when he feels that I'll not wake up hearing the voice of 'call ended'! Then he video calls me in the morning when he wakes up to see me sleeping and to fulfill my wish of 'I want to sleep watching you and want to open my eyes watching you!" so he does!

But calling and waking me up was his regular job!

How lovely na! He wakes me up with all his fondness for me. That morning, that call, the way he pampers me, the way he sees me, the way his eyes stare mine!

This was just the beginning of our day. Think how beautiful the days will be! So mesmerizing and amazingly beautiful.

At 8:00am, on the way to his college he'll call me and greet good morning in a package full of enthusiasm. We scarcely talk for 5minutes and he'll sprint into his college.

After my college, I come to my hostel and wait for him. Conventionally I fall asleep till the time he calls me. Then he has to wake me up againnnn. We talked for a while for like 15-20minutes, and then he left for his home leaving me alone behind. By the time he leaves I sleep again if Vedika has not yet arrived. As we've lunch together. Vedika and I have lunch, share what has happened in college, come back to our room, make it dark like night and swift ourselves into our favorite blankets.
(Madhu calling...)

Perfect timings of his always kept me after him. By now we'll sleep together. Unfortunately, in two different towns, in two different places, at two different houses, in two different rooms and on two different beds but on the same phone call, listening to each other's voice and breath.

I've my classes at 4:00 but I've my own customized alarm clock! Understood? Hahahaha... If he will read this statement he is definitely going to kill me for calling him a customized alarm clock. Okay, so it's obvious that he will wake me up.*(Wink)*

I buy tea and take it to my classes. Me, sir, brahmi and Nikhil will have tea and then my classes begin. Usually classes are for one hour but we sit there for 3 and a half hours or more.

After getting free from our classes, I and Brahmi will call our boyfriends. Oo yeah! Her boyfriend was my best friend. They both were classmates when they were in class 6th. He is Varin. Varin is a very clever student of our class just like Madeline. They call to talk but I call Madhu to inform him that my classes are finished and will call you in a while.

This was the only time when Madhu wait's for my class to over otherwise it's always me who is waiting for his call.

I and Brahmi hangout for some time and get back to our so called last destination of the day, for me it was my PG and for her it was her home. As soon as I reach my PG Vedika, Neelu di, Madhuri, Maitri everyone waits for me to come and then we share what we did the whole day..

I settle myself on swing and call him. We share about our day, we sing, he flirts, I share my philosophies, if it's raining then I'll try hard to convince him to bathe in rain. I'll go out for rainy drives and he'll possessively scream at me…Hayyyeee! We talk a lot in that particular phone call, we laugh a lot, we miss each other a lot, we talk about when we are going to meet.

After this also our day is yet not done! After this phone call he will send me for dinner and will force me to eat 3 tortillas. And, and not that if we are in a conference i.e. me, Varin and Madhu there are no chances of me winning and damnn if they stuck on one thing for me, THE GAME IS OVER! If they say you have to sit down and study, then I have to! There are no other choices left for me. If they say I've to eat four tortillas then I've to. But they both loved me a lot as so did I! And they get me into a lovely and sweet anger too! So that they both can breathe calmly after seeing my angry reactions, and in this way that annoying souls but the delightful ones make my day!

After dinner I and Vedika go for a 10 minutes drive that soothes our souls and makes us feel grateful for our existence. We sing along with the song played on phone or may be not played just singing with the environment out there. Some of the songs like Abhi na jao chhod kar, ye raatein ye mausam nadi ka kinara ye chanchal hawa…etc etc,
Then Varun calls us to catch up, we sit somewhere with him and after sometimes we get back to our pg.

Basically after 8 o'clock from nowhere any of us, except me, gets to the conversation of sexology, any topic ends with this and at last all we'll say is why do we end every topic after involving into this topic? *Laughters spread around!*

Everything has its end but not waiting for him! And he once again calls me at around 9:30-10:00pm when we walk towards his home from his shop. He specially takes this walk for me! If he is not at his shop then at that time he goes out to buy milk.

~

"INTEZAAR KI YE GHADI NA BEET-TI YUN…
AGAR SAMNE TERE JESA ISHQ KARNE VAALA MILTA
NAHI YUNN!"
-ITRA

10

<u>Three Days!</u>

Opppsss! Not of that menstrual cycle. But of his visiting cycle…hahaha sounds weird but don't get into that thought he doesn't come so often to meet me. I. It's just I tried to put my second sentence in rhythm with the first one…

It's like:

"HUM MILTE RAHE YUNHI BAAR BAAR…
TUJHE DEKHNE KO MANN CHAHTA HAI LAKH BAAR…
TEIR KAR KYA KARNA HAI ISS ISHQ KE SAMANDAR MEIN…
KABHI DOOB KE BHI DEKH LETE HAI ISKI GEHRAIYON
MEIN…!"
-ITRA

This time he came with his squad of girls. He and his four friends for their project work! As usual I went to meet him, hugged him, to make him sit behind me in my vehicle, he hugged me from behind while I was driving.

We went to a huge and beautiful garden. We sat below a tree. I was wearing a green check shirt with black ankle pant and he was in a baby pink shirt. He was leaning on a tree with his one leg folded above from his knee and the second was straightly aligned. I was leaning on his folded leg horizontally with the same position of legs: One folded and the other straight. His arms were around me and I tucked my hands in his hand which was surrounding me from the front.

He was listening to me and I was as usual chatter-patter. Then I noticed him, he has kept his eyes on me. That fool was watching me more than hearing what I'm saying. I slapped his jaw to break his view from me and to shift somewhere else. He was literally watching me like his thirsty eyes were waiting since years to satisfy his thirst. I literally felt like he was drinking me from his eyes and gulping me down…

Then I asked him "Where are you? What happened?" silent gestures, with my right eyebrow stretching it above. He smiled and he just shrugged his head and answered in the same gesture that "Nothing"
"Hungry?" I asked!
"Yes! Very much."

We went for lunch at a restaurant! We ordered two Punjabi dishes. By the time food was being prepared, the level of hunger had crossed another level. BIG FAT MICE running here and there. Right to left and back to right and round and round and round…UFFF!

There were four chapatis, 2 subjis', salad, lemon, papad, jeera-rice, Dal-Fry and butter milks in each of our plates. His plate had a vegetable sabji and a paneer sabji and my plate had only paneer-ki-sabji. It's not because I was special. It was because I don't like veggies!

We started but, we were aware about the tradition followed by 2 people when they are in a relationship. Of course it's because of love actually…but…

I was sitting on his right. The chapati was very hot so I waited for 20-30 seconds before tearing its first bite.
He took a bite of tortilla, dipped in sabji, made it in a temperature my mouth can handle by blowing air from his mouth on that bite and put it in my mouth.

                                        Chitra Nandola

We both were not having bites for ourselves instead giving bites to each other. That was more lovefull than having a bite of our own!

Even in daal-fry and jeera rice, he makes me eat with his spoon and my spoon was filled with bite for him.

We went back to the garden somewhere to have post lunch rest. This time when we were at the garden, my head was on his lap and he was actually making me sleep with his hand on my head and one hand holding my hand. That feeling wassssss!!!!

I slept as well without worrying about anything.

I miss his lap and that nap!

Then after sometime he woke me up. I woke up seeing him first when I opened my eyes! DREAMS COME TRUE!

We sat there for some time and I dropped him off at his hostel as he has to report there early.

We were so damn happy! No words can express the real happiness we felt that day being with each other.

There was no one to stop us that day for talking on phone calls that night but he was shy of people around him so he didn't. We slept after talking for some time.

~

Day-2

*"AYE KHUDA! MERI HAR SUBAH ITNI HI HASEEN KARDE...
USKA CHEHRA ROZZ AANKH KHULTE HI NAZAR
AAYE...AESA KOI JAADU KARDE!"*
-ITRA

I woke up and ran towards his hostel. I don't remember if I took a bath or not because he had to reach his industry at 10 o'clock and it was already 9 am. That place was 30-35 kms away from my place, so we went in a rush and in between we stopped at a place to have a cup of tea. Then he argued that now he'll drive and I'll sit behind him.

I said okay!

I sat behind him…kept my hands in the pockets of his jacket as it was freaking cold. I leaned on and held him tight! We even plugged earphones, one in his ear and one in mine.

Ye hasin waadiyann…ye khula aasman…aagaye hum kahan ae mere saathiyaa…- Song from 'Roza' a famous movie from the late 20th century…

Your Destination has arrived! Google map interrupted.

"Yet no one of your project partners has arrived, Madhu. Call them and ask them their whereabouts."

"Okay! Let me call them."

(Tried to call all the 3 of them)

"No one received the call Parthvi."

"So now what?"

"Nothing, let's wait for them to call what else!", *('He screamed in disguise)*

"Calm Down…"

We both were sitting on my vehicle in account of waiting for them to arrive.

I helped him by clicking some photos, we clicked a selfie together, ran after one another after teasing. Half an hour passed by but no hints of them coming.

(Madhu called them again)

One of them picked up and said we are on the way and about to reach in 10minutes.

He said, "Okay! I'm waiting" and hung up…

He hugged me and said, "Go and get ready, I'll call you when everything is over."

"No, let them come first, then I'll go"

"Are…it's okay bacha…you go and get freshen up."

"You sure?"
"Yup…now gooooo!"
"Okay! Okay!"
"See you"
"See you"
I went back to my Paying Guest. On the way I searched for them, in case I see them somewhere I can call him and tell him that they've reached here.
FINALLY AT MY PG!

I was literally tired, so settled myself on the floor. I kept my phone to charge and I was just about to sleep for 10-15minutes to take some rest…and my phone rang…

"Abbey yaar!" (I yelled)
I stood up to see who's calling. It was Madhu!
"Hello!"
"Hello Parthvi…"
"Yes Madhu!"
"My visit is over!"
What? Why so soon? I just reached here right now!
"So are you coming to pick me up?"
"Arey! How are those people going?"
"I don't know, maybe by a rickshaw or something…"
"Then get yourself into that rickshaw with them and I'll meet you somewhere on the way…"
"But I've not asked him about how they are leaving from here."
"Then at least ask them Madhu…"
"But how can I ask them…"
"It isn't a big deal yaar? Just ask them!"
Two of them are going together and the other two are going with their brothers."

"Okay then ask her if she could drop you somewhere in the middle of the city. I'll pick you from there."

"Parthvi...they've already left"

"WTF...Man! Okay I'm getting ready till the time if you get a rickshaw or something try to come okay"

"Okay"

How damn incapable this person is. He can't even ask his friends to drop him somewhere,

"I got ready! But in between he was continuously calling me.

It was so hot and sunny outside.

I went to that factory again to pick him up. No other option was left!

I reached there and gave him my vehicle to drive as I had no energy to drive again.

We went to a garden near a love temple. We sat there and then went to a restaurant for lunch. Damn my mood was devastated until I had some food.

I dropped him off at his hostel to have some rest and I got back to my PG.

We slept for an hour or two, got ready once again and went to Domino's. This time we were not alone, one of my roommates, DG was with us. We had pizzas and garlic bread sticks. Then we went somewhere for an outing, three of us were sitting below a tree.

At 11:00 I suggested to go back to our places but they did not agree and convinced me for a night out. We sat there for some time. I told them that the police will be patrolling, we cannot sit here for long and police came!

But the DG said no one will come, don't worry.

It was freaking cold too. I was feeling cold so I got myself a shawl too at the time of getting out of the room in case the temperature drops even more.

So Madhu wrapped me in that shawl and even he came into it. We were just sitting. DG was doing crazy things but both of us didn't speak a word. We were just enjoying being with each other…

Let's go to the outskirts of the city! DG suggested

No, I said, "We should not. I'm feeling cold. We should go back to our rooms.

But my suggestions and opinions were useless in front of them.

So I sat in the middle, DG was driving and Madhu was sitting behind me. The worst thing is when she drove the vehicle from a dangerous area of city, I was fucking scared! I yelled on her but Madhu stopped me, he covered me and him with that shawl! He hugged me tight so that I could feel some warmth against this cold.

He placed his face and head beside mine and kissed me twice on my cheek and on the side of my neck! That moment I seriously felt cozy. If he had done this before I must not have liked it but the situation didn't allow me to stop him doing that.

We reached that place. There were so many people around, the ambience was very impressive but the cold was massively affecting me from outside and from within.

DG went to give some order and we both were sitting on that wooden charpai. He was sitting in front of me and I was shivering a hell lot! I rested my head on his lap, lied on that charpai, and squeezed myself as much as I could. I was not at all in the position to talk or sit.

After sometime one of the bonfire places got empty. So we went there but nothing helped me to get myself some warmth. So I said again let's go to our places please. Otherwise I will die of cold.

Madhu said I'll not be permitted in my hostel right now. It's already 3!

I yelled at him that I told you both before only! I cannot even breathe right now. Do anything and help me to reach my room. You both want to roam, then go wherever you want to go. Drop me at my room.

But they fucking people planned to take him at our room.

What if our landlord got to know. I cannot take that risk. I don't want to risk my life. Fucking stop your bitchy ideas and think something else. I tried to convince them so hard, but the nuts didn't listen to me! Even Madhu wants to do as DG was saying and that bloody bastard ruined everything!

She secretly took him to our room! It was a nonsense idea and I don't even know what to do next! He went to freshen up himself and I was scared and worried sitting in the room and DG was talking with her boyfriend.

He came out. we set gadda(Mattresses) on the floor for us.

I was wrapped tightly in a thick blanket and he rested himself on my right. I was damn sleepy so I kept alarm and fell asleep. They both were going crazy and doing crazy things and I was not at all interested.

DG got a call and she started talking with her boyfriend and Madhu kept his one hand on me and fell asleep. I woke up at 4, before the sun went up and anyone could notice us. I tried to wake them up but they didn't even want to wake up now.

I got damn angry at them. I woke them up and we left the PG at 4:45am. We went to the garden beside the love temple.

Chitra Nandola

Now I was somewhat happy we clicked some pictures together and were kidding ourselves into the rides. DG became our cameraman and clicked photographs for us. The photographs were damn cute but the scars were damn deep!

We got ourselves some breakfast and went to our rooms at 8am.
We got ready, slept for some time and planned to catch up again for the movie.
"MISSION IMPOSSIBLE-FALLOUT" is one of the best movies I've seen. Incredible movie, Tom Cruise is his favorite hero damn handsome!
Then we got back to our PG as I wanted to get ready for the photoshoot.
I wore an orange saree and black bellies. He was in white shirt. Again DG became our cameraman and we had beautiful memories together. That place was very beautiful. Then we went to the temple of that place to find a change room and washroom as I needed to change my clothes now.
That room was so dark and scary, I told DG to stand outside and not to go anywhere. Somehow I managed to get change, trying to overcome the darkness and the fear!

Then we went to a very famous place. Iit was a garden restaurant with a disco and a *kat-putli* (Puppet) show.

First we sat on the swing and behaved like kids while sitting on kids rides. Then we went to the disco room. We did a couple dance there and many more. It was the first time that Madhu has danced in front of me. We enjoyed it for 45minutes or more and went for dinner. We had to wait in a long queue for our chance. Now, we were hungry like demons! We urged the manager to get our turn as soon as possible but he was more into managing people turn by turn. So unfortunately we have to wait there till our turn comes.

After dinner, our battery was low so we reached our rooms as soon as possible and slept even without talking. Just a good night nothing else!
Next day morning we met, we roamed in the city for sometime and we left for lunch from where DG joined us again. We ate lunch and went to a beautiful garden, sat there for sometime below a tree. DG got a call and she got busy with it.

Madhu rested his head on my lap and held one of my hands.We both were mum(Quite) as we wanted to feel the presence of each other.
At 6' o'clock we went to Madhu's hostel and took his bags and dropped him off at his bus.
Now you can imagine how difficult that bye would be! I was unable to speak a single word.
THEN HE LEFT THE CITY…!

~

"INN HASIN MULAKATO KA EK YAHI NUKSAN HAI...
USS SHAQS KE JAANE KE BAAD SAB ADHURA-ADHURA
SA LAGTA HAI!"
-ITRA

                                                            Chitra Nandola

11

Birthday!

Birthdays are damn special for me and unlucky for him.
Every time I cannot be with him on his birthday but I try to make it special at 12:00am.

I usually make cake out of my chocolates; get ready in beautiful attire and with tints of kajal, mascara and open hairs!
I video call him, he receives from his bathroom; I and my roommates cut his cake and wish him happy birthday. Then we chat late at night and sleep around at 2:00 am- 3:00am.

Next day morning I wished him again when he called me to wake me up. But the worst part is he never communicates and even picks up my call when he is surrounded with people.

No doubt he has lesser friends and not even a single loyal friend but still he chooses not to talk while he is with them. He doesn't like teasing and all, so he tries to avoid our topic in front of them.

Even If I ask him at night, how was your day? Who all were there? Did you enjoy it or not? What have you done all day? But he will never explain the whole thing to me.

~

My birthday!! My last birthday in this city as I'm shifting to Calicut next year! So basically I wished it to be the best! But it was more than just BEST!

JUST BEST! Yes you read it correctly!

First of all at 12am, me and my roomies went to a crossing to cut my cake. An awesome cake. We clicked crazy photos there on the footpath on the divider, some of them sitting on my lap, cake cream spread over my face, screaming and running after each other. We reached the room and cleaned ourselves. My phone was ringing continuously maa-paa, siblings, cousins, friends, relatives, everyone was calling me. I cleaned myself and washed my hair. We all sat for gossip and I was also receiving all the calls then finally all we slept.

In the morning I got ready and was waiting for Varin and Madhu. Yes they both were coming here for my birthday…! I was very excited for the day.

First Vedika warmly hugged me, wished me and then I went for a bath.

I wore a floral gown of pink color, and kept my hair half open. Vedika helped me with the eyeliner, kajal and lipstick.

Vedika had an important lecture that day so she went for it while I was waiting for Madhu to call me after entering the city!

Landlords, roomies and others calls were attended!

("Madhu Calling…!" Screen Flashed)

You reached? *I asked in brightly widened eyes with my 32 teeth smile.*

"Yes,come soon! I've an emergency. Nature's call!"

"Okay okay I'm coming.Wait there"

I drove my vehicle in such an excited and happy mood that I covered a 15 minutes drive under 8.

He hugged me, wished me, and I took him to the nearest mall.Best I can think of at that very time and instant moment!

He rushed to the washroom!

I was waiting outside. As the previous hug was not very satisfying (Wink), I need a longer one this time!

He came out and hugged me tighter. I felt that love, I felt that warmth, I felt my heart out happiness. I felt him there, I felt us there, I felt the truth there and his adorable care and happiness! *I think you felt that feeling no? Too adorable…cannot digest (Wink)!*

We went to my college as I wanted to meet my classmates, faculties and all the supporting staff members. Supporting staff members were more excited for me to meet them on this day! Because I loved them and they loved me even more.

I and Madhu went there. Distributed chocolates, seek blessings and best wishes by touching feets of supporting staff members and faculties.

I found them around the college so that I don't miss out on anyone because I didn't want to!

We even met our college's favorite food stall uncle.

While departing from there we took another road which had less traffic and can give us some privacy.

We stopped at a point in a small street. We stood there and talked about some teasing things, hugged each other more. He kissed my left cheek, right cheek, head and nose. *No words to explain how it felt!*

He grabbed me and trapped me in his arms and was teasing me, being romantic…

But the most funny thing was the moment someone passed by us he left me in a fear and that happened more than 10 times! So I was laughing out loud holding my stomach and he was staring at me in anger. We left the place.

Varin called me!

"Yes Varinnnnn, have you reached?" *I shouted in excitement!*

"Yeah!" *He said*

"Okay then where are you?"

"I've already reached Shivaji road."

"Okay we'll be reaching there in 10 minutes…

Meanwhile we reached Shivaji road, he left from there to the nearby reliance mall!

(Madhu called Varin) "Hey Varin! Where are you standing. Why aren't you visible?"

"I've reached the Reliance mall. Come here."

Madhu said okay and hung up.

"He has reached the reliance mall." *Madhu said*

"Why? I was…...."

He cut me in between and said, "It is the same reason I wanted to go there."

"Acha okay!" *I exclaimed*

~

Did you know I passed by Madhu's shop twice today. But I saw him neither of the time, So sad no? May not be my luck today!

**"*AANKHEN TARAS GAYI AAJ USKO DEKH NE KE LIYE...*
VO CHAND TO JESE GAYAB HI HO GAYA MUJHSE AANKHE
CHURAKAR! "
-ITRA

Okay back to the story!

So we reached where Varin was. He wished me too! He was quite enthusiastic today, *usually he never is! (Wink)*

We went to a nearby garden tripling on my scooter.

We sat there on a bench and were bitching about college.

Bhrami arrived in a white top and blue denim.

We exchanged greetings and sat on the bench. Clicked some pictures, and continued our gossip…

Vedika arrived from college...

Varin and Bhrami went for a long drive, and Vedika went to our PG keeping Madhu waiting outside the society till the time we came back.

Vedika freshened up and got ready. My concentration was completely on Madhu that he was waiting for me.

Vedika did my touch up too… *"A possessive best friend"*

We came out in my vehicle, made Madhu sit behind Vedika and me as I was driving.

They kept me waiting outside with a promise not to come inside. Both went to a bakery.

They came out with a cake. probably I was looking like a huge 1 kg cake.

We went back to that garden and even Bhrami and Varin came back from a long drive after sometime.

According to Vedika and Madhu's plan they made me sit on a bench, Madhu bent down on his knees.

Ooo Baapreee what's happening? What is he doing? Did he lose his nuts or I lost mine? Is this really happening?

Madhu and Vedika asked me to open the rose!

I did! AND THERE WAS A STERLING SILVER RING! *Speechless! Shocked!*

I Love you! Will you be mine for forever? *He asked*

I turned towards Vedika, She was like Say yes, Say yes…

Yeah…*I said*

He slided that ring into my finger, I stood up and jumped over him to hug him tight. He lifted me up when I hugged him to get that feel harder. My eyes were wet and his eyes too!

A DAY BEFORE THE BIG EVENT! (COINCIDENCE)

Vedika, I should buy something for Madhu no?

"I want to make him feel more special."

"Yes you should!" *She said.*

We discussed many things and at last we were stuck on a ring.

We went to a mall.

We bought a plain gold plated sterling silver ring for him.

Size? *Vedika asked me*

"Two size bigger than my finger.", *I said*

We found the right size for him then bought a ring box.

I was so damn excited for the day!

So If he brought a ring for me and even I bought a ring for him, Was it a coincidence?

But deep down Vedika was a mere truth hider. She didn't discussed anything about this to me and we thought it's a coincidence.

It was my turn now!

I bent down on my knees, with a shivering voice and teary eyes.

You have to say something. You cannot give him a ring this way! *Vedika said*

I was silent for 2 minutes frozen at the same position.

"I Love you Madhu! I cannot explain how it is feeling right now but it's pure without any scars. Will you be mine forever? Will you love me forever?"

Yess! *He said with brighter eyes.*

I slid the ring over his ring man.

Varin, Bhrami and Vedika were taking pictures…

Vedika opened the box and it was a chocolate cake with two teddy bears assuming one me and another Madhu, and a name on it; which says "PARDHU" i.e Parthvi + Madhu! An un-elaborative smile!

We blushed.

We cut the cake, I gave him a piece of cake and applied cream from my fingers to both of his cheeks.

He gave me a big piece that I was not able to altogether chew it too. That crazy monkey….

We both shared cake with brahmi, Vedika and Varin.
Had to buy a water bottle to clean our faces because we all were sticky.
"Let's have some lunch now, everyone must be hungry."
"Okay what you all want to eat? Pizza, Pasta, Punjabi, Gujarati?"
What do you want to eat, it's your birthday. We'll have anything. *They proclaimed.*
"I...I want to go to dominos."
"Okay then let's go!"

Vedika, I & Madhu on my vehicle; and Bhrami & Varin on Brahmi's vehicle.

We got settled in a table exactly in front of the counter.
Varun arrived and wished me and settled down beside

Vedika. I told them if anyone could bring some cold drinks from outside when I approached to order pizza.
I ordered 5-6 pizzas including Margherita, Italian, onion and cheese, and garlic bread sticks.

Madhu served everyone a glass of soft drink when pizzas came.
We all ate pizzas like animals. Everyone was damn hungry!
Then we went to our secret garden back to spend some time together and to create more crazy memories.

We clicked some pictures on swings and benches and Madhu lifted me up in his arms, Varin held me by his hand around my neck, Gandhiji's three monkey poses with Bhrami and Vedika.

Bhrami and Varin wanted to spend some time together so they went for a long drive on the highway.
Varun was also in some work that day and he was also not with us after lunch.

I, Vedika and Madhu were in that garden now.

Vedika went to play with swing and gave us some private time. Although it was not required no doubt but she alleged a lot and went off from there.
We both were sitting first, I've spring in me which makes me jump off every time I sit somewhere. So I was getting up repeatedly and he was making me sit back. Then he got tired of making me sit again and again so he pulled me from my wrist, settled me in his lap and surrounded me with his arms so that I couldn't get up again.

I was talking and talking and talking and as usual he was listening and smiling and smiling and just smiling!
Then he took out something from his pocket. I was wondering what he was doing.
"Close your eyes." *He said*
And I did.

He put something around my neck and said open your eyes now.
OOO MYYY GODDDDD! HE BROUGHT MY FAVORITE LOCKET.
It was looking damn beautiful as of course because he tied it around my neck.

After sometime around 5:30 or something Varin and Bhrami arrived.
Then my childhood friend/bro came. Veeru wished me and hugged me.
But it was almost 6:15 by now and Madhu had to leave us as he had his bus at 7'o clock.

I and Madhu left for his bus and rest everyone stayed there in that garden.
We were driving by the highway, he was driving and I was sitting behind leaned on him, hugging him, resting myself on his back to *feel him, his warmth for the last moments I got with him. I was crying from inside, I'm*

gonna miss him a lot and a lot. I don't want him to go. I want to stay with him. I want to be with him. I want to bury my head into his chest. I want to hug him tight forever. I don't want him to leave me like this. I'll miss him. Madhu please don't go, my mind was provoking these thoughts again and again…

Madhu…
"Please don't go…please"(*hugging him tighter*)
"We are going to meet soon, don't worry"
"We reached there."

Bus was on time!
He sat inside the bus. I drove along with his bus till some distance.
Please don't go, Please. I'll miss you.
The bus passed by me and he left me there. I was not at all in the mood now. I didn't want him to leave me like this.
I went back to that garden; everyone was waiting for me. I bought a cheese puff for Varin, he was also leaving at 9.

I reached the garden.
Veeru, Vedika and Bhrami came to me.
I asked where Varin was.
They both were like he left. He was getting late.
"But he didn't even meet me at last, didn't even call me or text me. He cannot go like this. You are lying. I know."
"No we are not." *Vedika said*
"Seriously? *I asked.*"
"Yes!" *They said*
My mood changed from worse to worst in microseconds.
Varin came forward from behind a tree, when he saw me like this.
Hey, I'm here, I haven't left yet. How could I without greeting you last bye?
And I got that smile back!

We all went to my classes with cake to meet my sir.
I touched his feet to be blessed. He wished me my success.
I cut the cake there and made him eat a piece forcefully because being a singer he would not like to spoil his throat.

Then I insisted him to sing a song for me as it was my birthday.
Actually sir is only 1 or 2 years older than us so sometimes we can ask him something like this, he doesn't mind much if the situation is correct.
So he sang "Tera Fitoor"…

His voice is damn soothing. It melts your heart in no time. I love his voice, his skills, his grips, I love to listen to his songs again and again.
Then sir told Bhrami to play guitar and *I said,* "sir Veeru sings very well…lets collab them both…"
"Okay…" *Sir said*

They both sang together "Oo ri Chiraiya"
This hour made my day again. I'm a fan of music, songs, instruments, everything. My moods depend on which song is playing right now. Songs can change my moods instantly.

Then we dropped Varin at his stop. He hugged me and Brahmi. He shook hands with Vedika and Veeru.
And he left.

After that even Bhrami had to reach home so she greeted me and went off wishing me my birthday for the last time.

Vedika, Veeru and I went to a fast food shop to buy some food for my college classmates as we've planned to meet in a very famous and huge garden, where people come and sit at nights too.

We made a round and settled ourselves. I was very angry with them that day. It was my birthday and I was forcing them to come and meet me… like what, isn't it their responsibility for this day?
But then after sometime everything got normal.

They all brought cake for me. Cake with three creamy cats on it. I cut my third cake of my day.
And we ate burgers, hot dogs, sandwiches etc, I bought them all.
They were eating more wildly than we ate in the afternoon. Hahaha…
It was 10:15 by now and maa-paa called me to ask my whereabouts.
I told them I'm about to leave in 15minutes.
They said okay be quick! *And end the call…*
"I've to leave now. It's my mumma papa's order!"
We all should also leave now everyone said.

We all departed on our ways.
On our way to pg, I and Vedika dropped Veeru at his flat.
Finally we reached PG and were tired af!
I directly lied down on the floor for 5-7 minutes and meanwhile called mom-dad.

Even Madhu was popping messages and calling to ensure I reached PG or not!
I dropped a message to him that I've reached and my call is on with my mom-dad. Will talk to you later.

I explained everything I did that day and happened to me that day except that exchange of rings and hugs and kisses or that my and Madhu's moments. But they knew that Madhu and Varin came here for my birthday.
And my day ended with gossips of my roomies as usual, I hugged Vedika and fell asleep. *(Peace)*

I WAS IN A MESMERIZED MODE! I WAS VERY HAPPY, DANCING, CRAZY JERK, LOST, WONDERING, SMILING, BLUSHING, RECALLING EVERYTHING!

~

"BEHADD KHUSHI THI...
KII HADD HO GAYI...
JISKE HASNE SE MOTI CHALLAKTE THE UN LABON SE VO
MUSKAN NAM HOGAYI...!"
-ITRA...

12

<u>Difficulties ruin our lives and lead we departed!</u>

No one in his family or among his friends was pushing him towards his career. I was the only one who had now become a headache for him! I wanted him to be at least that much successful that whenever his parents need anything or ask him for anything, he doesn't need to refuse them.

All my speeches, my words, my anger, my lectures, my efforts of making him understand things were mere waste! Nothing worked at all! He had no idea what he was doing with his future! Destiny, fate, everything comes with the collaboration with karma of your past life and this life! Some things are pre-decided but that doesn't mean that you stop making efforts! That's the mere sign of losing your opportunities, in losing your trust from your own! Can you imagine dropping BBA with a collection of 7 KTs! How can someone be so irresponsible! So damn irresponsible! Bloody jerk!

Months and months passed away like this! I'm not saying he didn't try but he didn't give his 100%. Television, serials, movies, mobile games, chatting with me, calling me, hanging out with friends, that's it!

At first I felt that if I stop messaging him and talking on phone calls, he will be hurt and start doing things in fear of losing me! But naaahhh! Plan failed!

Then I started asking him every day what he did today? In pampering tones and all! But he got tired of giving answers every day and started behaving rudely with me! Instead of understanding what is good for him and what is bad, he started maintaining distance from me like I'm his enemy!

And this behavior made me angrier! My headache became my regular partner! My wait for him became my basics! My every little efforts like talking to my dad for his job, arranging him somewhere in my firm, searching a good job for him, talking to different-different places for him, arranging something in his locality for him everything became seamless, unworthy, of no meaning! I ran here and there begging for some job for him but he didn't make an effort to walk a single step with me!

I even suggested him to work in his own shop for some days, try to learn the things, how accounts are maintained, how liabilities are paid, how customers are greeted, how they are served, how to clean the shop, how to manage and handle the things! But nothing seems to be working! Not a single effort from his side!

It hurts a lot when you are the only one who is making an effort in the relationship and other people don't give a thought to it! Not a single thought! My crying, weeping, headache, stress, weight gains, irregular stress eating, everything started increasing! But he didn't cared! He wants to sit back and relax! No forecasting of future, no tension about future! Nothing! I was dying for him every day but I got to know one thing that even if I die he will not even give half a percent more to his efforts. He will be the same as he is right now! Because he didn't wanted to do the things, he wants to succeed but he doesn't wanted to work hard, he wants to depend on his destiny but not want to create his own! He imagines himself somewhere but he doesn't try to get that thing in his life! That hurts the most that your dreams are being killed, every time he kicks off one of his own dreams! He never thought that this sitting ideal with a 12th pass degree will kill our relationship! For me this time was the worst. My bad! My every effort was murdered! My three and a half year old relationship sank into the ocean of truth of life! My love for him was still alive but his life-boat on my way had become a sharp knife for my heart! That knife which has blood stains of my dreams, my future life with him, my past years relationship, his love, his care, his own career, his own dreams, his impression, his trust, **EVERYTHING! EVERYTHING!**

Now for me as well as him it was being necessary to end this drama of relationship! I was totally became a destroyed person and the only thing I admire about that phase was I didn't get involved into stupid habits of drinking or smoking. The end was hardest for me. But I found him smiling after this. No doubt he must have been through hard times. I agree with it! But after some countable days he was stable but me? Yes exactly what you thought! **AND I STILL FALL FOR HIM!**

I lost my trust in relationships, love, break ups! Statements like I'll never leave you, I can't live without you, I'll love you for my whole life, I promise to be with you forever; I love you forever ever and ever, I'm nothing without you, You are my soul my heartbeat. My sweetheart, my cute baby!

Everything felt to be FAKE, UNREALISTIC, FAKE PROMISES, USING OF SOMEONE'S EMOTIONS AND FEELINGS, MAKING SOMEONE MENTALLY & PHYSICALLY; AND EMOTIONALLY WEAK! IT'S AN ACT OF KILLING SOMEONE'S TRUST, IT IS AN ACT OF MURDERING SOMEONE'S FEELINGS AND EMOTIONS!

It has been 3-4 days we haven't talked so one day I messaged him. He hadn't replied till evening, so I called him. He didn't even received my call so I chose to wait for him. I won't be able to sleep till 4am as I didn't receive a single response from him.

Next day morning, when I woke up, no messages, no calls from him! I lost my patience and sent a 5-6 liner message in anger!
He has developed a habit of waking up after 10am so when I was in office I got a reply around 10:30am! That reply!
I literally became numb! My hand on my forehead! my headache started hitting me hard! I was unable to understand what just happened! It took me 5-7 minutes to recognize what just happened!

I called Heer from my cabin.
"Heer! Heer! Heer! Do you know what?" I, Heer and Aadi were on a conference call at that time as when I called them, they both were already on a call!

Aadi is a best friend of heer from her college. He is tall and has a very good personality. Even my bond with him was too good. He is a smart guy full of knowledge! And he knew what was going on between me and Madhu!

I was stammering and unable to speak a word! Heer and Aadi were like, "Tell us what happened? Why are you stammering? What is scaring you? Anyone said something to you?"

I ran out of my office, my tears were not stopping at all!

"Heer!" *(I Muttered)*
"Heer, he was not replying to me, didn't picked up my calls, we haven't talked since days that's why I messaged him in anger today morning when I woke up and now his reply came."

Heer: What did you messaged?
"I did a text message that, "At least, pick up my call or reply to my message when you get free. No messages, no replies. I'm not your enemy. Why are you doing this to me? Go to hell!

And…

Heer: And what? What did he reply?

Me: Heer! Heer! He sent me two emoji of Middle finger. He meant to say fuck you! Like it was all my fault!

Heer and Aadi: Calm down first! Call him and add him in this conference call.

(I called 2-3 times but he didn't pick up…)

"He is not picking up my call!"

Heer: Let me try!

(He didn't even receive Heer's call!)

Heer: Didn't pick up mine too!

Aadi: Let me try!

Aadi: No response!

Heer: I'm messaging him!

Heer Messaged Madhu: Call me as soon as possible otherwise you know we'll not take much time in finding you mumma's number or dad's number!

Madhu messaged me: I'm Brushing, call you in a while!

Me: Heer he messaged me. He is saying that he is brushing and will call in a while.

(His call came after a while)

Madhu: Hello!

Heer: Why did you message her like that?

Madhu: I did it by mistake. I was clicking on emoji near to it but by mistake I clicked on that emoji.

Heer: Don't you re-check your message before sending? Like can you see what emoji you are using? You making us fool?

Madhu: No No seriously trust me.

Heer: And why are you not replying or not receiving her calls or even our calls?

Madhu: I'm not well since a week that's why my mumma is not allowing me to take my cell phone.

Heer: You are not well since a week? What happened to you?

Madhu: I'm suffering from a cough & cold.

Heer: But it's normal at least you can reply or inform us and you haven't felt this much sick in the last three and a half years? You've never done this in years! Then why now?

Madhu: Because I'm not getting to my normal condition this time otherwise I have a quick recovery.

Heer: Madhu please don't lie now!

Madhu: I'm telling the truth!

Heer: Okay tell me one thing! Do you want to continue this relationship? Tell me whatever truth is, Parthvi will never message you again if you say no!

Madhu: Actually, one of my aunts told my mumma that I'm uploading pictures on my friend's birthday. Recently it was Bhoomi's birthday at that time and mumma scolded me a lot. She is not accepting my friends too if they are girls!

Heer: You should have thought about this earlier and even Parthvi warned you that if your mumma will not allow then we end our relationship it's better to end earlier than after a long time. And every time you tell her that you will convince your mom-dad, right?

Madhu: Right, but...

Heer: But what? Then why are you giving these reasons now? Is she a toy that you come and play with her anytime you want and then leave her when she is not needed huh?

Ok, so, what are you finalizing now?

Madhu: Give me some time. I'll think and inform you.

Heer: Finalize your decision and call us by evening!

Madhu: Hmm okay!

(Madhu hangs up the call)

I was still mum! No words, no thoughts, no convo, nothing was coming into my mind!

Heer: Parthvi, don't worry. You chill and complete your office hours. We'll discuss this in the evening. Okay?
Me: hmm…
Heer & Aadi: Bye take care…
Me: hmm bye.

~

My mind was continuously evaluating what his decision would be! He had no idea in which stage I was! And I didn't even want him to know that. I don't know why I don't want him to know that but I don't wanted to express anything to him. What I'm feeling. What I've gone through. What I was trying to do, anything! There was nothing left to explain! Not even a single word is worth explaining to him! What-so-ever his decision would be, I'll accept it! But this black stain will never vanish! NEVER EVER!

" DHEERE-DHEERE VISHVASH MERA KHO RAHA THA…
PATA BHI NAHI CHAL RAHA THA KI KUCH KSHANO ME YE
KYA HO RAHA THA!"
-ITRA

~

"SHAAM HONE WALI HAI…
IMTEHAN KI GHADI AANE WALI HAI…
TU DIL CHHOTA NA KAR MERI JAAN…
USKI HAAN HI AANE WALI HAI!"
-ITRA

Heer called him in the evening. I was not in the conference.

"THAMJA AE DIL VO BOHOT ACHA BANDA HAI…
TUJHE YUNN ISS BAAR KOI TODKE NAHI JAANE VAALA
HAI!"
-ITRA

(Heer called me)
Heer: Hii Parthvi! What are you doing?
Me: Hey!
Heer: I talked with him…
Me: Hmm… What did he said?

(Heer's call recording with Madhu)

Madhu: Hello
Heer: Hello… Yes!
Madhu: Sorry please! I don't mean that! I'm really very sorry! It's not that I don't want to talk to her, before some days I approached her and I messaged her.
Heer: Yeah… "Good morning have a nice day"
Madhu: Yes I'm talking with her. It's not that I don't talk with her! But I'm unable to talk. I'm fighting a lot at my home. Yesterday only mom was asking me why Parthvi is calling you these many times(I just called twice that too in intervals), so I told mumma that she is just calling for gossiping with me. Every friend calls me. They are my friends obviously they'll call me to talk with me. It's not like that mumma. In that thing too I had a big fight with my mumma. I'm not well too and plus all these things are adding up on me. Sorry yaar… I'm sorry!
Heer: Don't say sorry again and again. It's just I cannot see her crying every day and I want to know your side of this situation. I don't know what is going on in your life. I just know your chats and what Parthvi says to me. So if I'm not knowing what is going on in your side, how will I understand the things.
Madhu: Even mumma was asking me why are you not recovering. Why is this fever not going? For two weeks my fever has been coming and going, coming and going. It went away for two days and came again on the third day.

Heer: Hmm

Madhu: We showed my report to one of the Dr. he said it's just a viral fever. But I'm not feeling like this is viral fever.

Heer: Hmmm

Madhu: Today we are visiting another Dr. for this…

Heer: Do you have fever today?

Madhu: No, not today, but my head is aching a lot. When I woke up in the morning I got this headache! That's why I wanted to send something else but mistakenly I sent her this! When I woke up I saw her long message. I didn't even read that message. I just read "go to hell-go to hell"

Heer: Hmm… But how can this error occur?

Madhu: Doesn't it happen by mistake sometimes?

Heer: Leave that message, we have to see rest. I'm asking you a straightforward question," Do you want to stay in this relationship or not?

Madhu: No now I don't want to be in this relationship anymore, leave this now!

Heer: Why?

Madhu: I don't want to continue this relationship now. Yesterday my dad was working on my PC at that time also I was about to be caught as that PC has a folder of our photos.

Heer: See about getting caught by your parents! When you both came into a relationship at that time you knew that one day you have to tell this to your parents, right?

Madhu: Yes!

Heer: Then why are you giving this reason that I don't want to be caught by my parents that's why I want to leave her?

Madhu: I want to tell this at home but I don't know what will happen after that! I'm afraid.

Heer: That fear was with you from the first day of relationship and now also you are giving the same reason! Then you didn't realize that thing in these three years or more, not in the first month and neither in the last month of the relationship? That this thing is not possible for you to inform at home? On what basis have you been with her since these three and a half years? If I'm in a relationship with someone, I've to tell this at home. So if you both are in a relationship then one thing you should've fixed in your mind that you have to inform this at home! And now you are denying because of this reason that you cannot inform about this relationship at home! Then why were you with her for these three years?

Heer: Answer!

Madhu: What should I answer now?

Heer: You don't have an answer to this question because this reason of yours is not at all valid! You should have known this before coming into relationship with her if you were serious about this relationship! You were serious about her in these three years?

Madhu: Obviously I was!

Heer: Then didn't you realize this thing in these last three years? Now today you are afraid of fights with your mom and dad? You've to inform this at your home, right? If these problems had not arrived in your lives right now then you would have continued this relationship for two years more! And then in the end moment when we have to inform this thing at our home at that time you would wake up and tell us that now I cannot tell this at my home then what'll be her situation? Didn't you spoiled 3 years of someone's life? You think by yourself, even you've a sister at your home!

Now you don't have any answer, what will I do with her now? How will I handle her? She is my sister, you are an outsider. No matter how close you were to her, you'll leave her in this condition but I cannot. She is my sister! We have to take care of her anyhow, right! She is living in such a worst condition, what Madhu will be doing right now? Why is he not replying? Why is he doing this to me? You left her after living three years in relation with her! Your work is done! Who will take care of her now? You boys before doing something like this think once that you too have a sister and how will you feel when someone

Chitra Nandola

will do something like this to her? How will you feel when someone she loves will leave her giving this reason to her? Doesn't matter how serious you are, at last you gave her a ring too, not even 1% of it is giving any meaning to it now! When you don't want to get married to her then why were you in a relationship with her? There is no meaning of your past fights, of your single promise, of a single I love you, from what you are saying right now! You have not even kept that much that she can introduce you as just a friend of hers! She cannot even call you as a friend if she meets you someday somewhere! You said a clear NO on my face that you don't want to be in relationship with her! If you've given me reason that you don't like her nature then also I would have accepted your reason but you are giving reason that you cannot inform at home that's why you want to leave her! We would not take even two minutes to inform this at your home! I don't want to ruin your life, I've to handle and take care of my sister! I don't want to ruin someone's life! And you have already spoiled three years of Parthvi's life! Three years is not a small thing! She has much more feelings for you, I don't know about you. For you saying no is so easy! It's very difficult for her to say no! She has to answer every one of us! You know that every cousin knows about your and her relation! She is answering everyone even to me! If someday I ask her in anger about this she has to answer even me! Still she is agreeing that you must have mistakenly sent her that message! What respect did you give to her? If you can't be respectful towards this bond of yours at least respect that person! And still if you don't want to be with her tell her on her face that you don't want this relationship! At least we will take care of her and she can rid herself from this relationship! Don't hang her in the middle of this relation! If you don't want to stay in this relationship then say clearly that you don't want to continue this relation anymore! We'll take care of her. She is not alone. We all are with her! There is nothing affecting you in just messaging once to her no matter how much fever you have. At least you can inform her once! Even my father was not well but that doesn't mean that he will not talk with us!

Even we all are falling sick! And you are talking with me right now because we warned you that we'll call your mother otherwise today also you wouldn't have called back! Right? This is not the first time, since last 2-3 times you have not called back us, not to Aadi, me or even Parthvi! If you don't want to continue this relationship, say NO clearly on my face! She will not call you or message you and even if you don't try to get in touch with her, us, Ashwini or any of our friends! Don't even try to contact any of us! Tell me NO if you are not interested in this anymore! You are not even getting affected by any of these things. Say NO directly, right in front of my face! You wasted three years of my sister's life! At least her Ex was good who told her on her face that he is getting married to someone else as her family is forcing him! You don't even have that much guts that you say on her face that you want to discontinue this relationship! If I wouldn't have called you today then this must be going on as it is and she will be dying every day! She is studying as well as doing her job right now! She is not concentrating even 1% in it right now! She is awake whole days and nights! Madhu will reply to me, Madhu this, Madhu that! A week or so ago, one day I called her in the morning. I talked with her, calmed her mind and then she slept on my call and her headache healed! Don't only you have problems in life, everyone have problems! Learn to at least understand someone! Once I told her that don't pressurize Madhu for his career, she stopped pressurizing you! Try to at least understand something, don't ruin someone's life like this! Tell her on her face that you don't want to be with her! And she has this much in her that if you will once say no to her she will not call you or message you! She has this sanskar in her! She will not even annoy you after that! None of us wants to ruin your life! But at least don't spoil my sister's life! She has tolerated you for three years no matter what you said and told her to do, no matter however time you insulted her! No doubt even she behaved worse sometimes! But she has taken care of this thing, so even she has this right to know that you don't want to be with her anymore! At least think little about someone and say sorry if you feel so! So that at least we can feel that you as a person was good! My maternal uncle told this thing before that Madhu is not a good person and he will not stay forever with Parthvi! And even you must be knowing this thing that she got a call from my uncle! At that time I didn't believed, I was thinking that no Madhu is a good person, He is a good person! You remember the first time you told her I love you? Even that time we were thinking that Madhu cannot do this thing. He is a good person! Even though she told you that you are a very good person you cannot do this! Remember you were sitting with Vickey at that time? At least respect that thing that how much we trust you! For me, Ashwini, Ritika didi, is it easy to trust you for this? Is it easy for us to give you our sister? If we were trusting on you then and only then we have kept her with you na? If I tell Parthvi to end this relationship with you she doesn't have the guts to say no to me! And you also know that thing, that if any of us me, Ashwini or Ritika didi will tell her once to not to talk to you, she will stop talking to you! We are supporting you, at least inform us if you cannot inform her! At least inform any one of us so that we can look after her! You leave her, we stop looking after her, then what will she do with her life? You are doing these much to her and you know what Ritika didi fought with her before some days that you are not supporting him in his hard time! He has problems, you support him, he is trying to focus somewhere that's why Parthvi was supporting you this much at that time too! Ritika di scolded her taking your side! At least respect that! At that time Parthvi's mind was drawn more, then also she did these much for you! It is becoming easy for you boys to leave any girl like this! Think something at least, it's her life! You didn't like it and you left! You have problems at your home and you left her! When our family will be suffering from problems at that time how it will feel if she left you saying I want to discontinue and don't you ever message me or call me! Get out of our life! Will it be feasible? You don't even take two minutes in spoiling a girl's life! We don't say anything to you, why? Is it difficult for me to find your mumma's number right now? Just answer me this much! If I want to find your mumma's number or papa's number will I be unsuccessful in finding one? I will not take even two minutes to do that and I even have very beautiful pictures of yours as a witness! If I want to ruin your life it will not take me two minutes to do that! But I don't want to do that! Why should I spoil your life? I should look after my sister or think of your toxicity? If you don't do anything in your life just be a nice person and don't spoil someone's life! This is a simple and straightforward thing that doesn't spoil someone's life! Are you now answering anything? Do you have something to say anymore?

Madhu: What should I say now?

Heer: Do you want to be with her or not? Just say yes or no? Then I'll cut the call and will not tell you anything after that! And don't be afraid of us that we will do something to you and your life! Answer me what the truth is!

~

"KEHNE KO KYA THA USKE PASS KYUNKI USKO PATA THA VO GALAT HAI...
JO KIYA AUR JO HUA USME GALAT TO VAHI HAI...
WO JANTA THA KI EK DIN AISA ZAROOR AAYEGA...
LEKIN KYA ANJAAM LEKE AAYEGA USKA ANDAZA SHAYAD USKO NAHI THA!"
-ITRA

13

<u>And I loved you for thousand years!</u>

*"BEPANAAH ISHQ THA, BEPANAAH ISHQ HAI AUR
BEPANAAH RAHEGA...
MERI IN NIGAHON MEIN TERE LIYE ISHQ BEKARAAR
RAHEGA...
MUJHE TERE ISHQ KARNE YA NA KARNE SE FARQ NAHI
PADTA...
YE MERA ISHQ HAI, MERE LIYE KHUDGARZ HI RAHEGA!"*
-ITRA

*"Yeh soch kar kuch palon ki mohabbat kar baithe...
Wo hum pe pal do pal ki mohabbat ka ehsaan kar bethe...*

*Wo masoom se palon ko khushnuma kar bethe...
wo hum pe pal do pal ki mohabbat ka ehsaan kar baithe...*

*Sochte the ki puri zindagi aapki bahon mein bethe rahe...
Par aap to...bas
Wo hum pe pal do pal ki mohabbat ka ehsaan kar bethe...*

*Bade hi pyaar se is haqiqat-ae-aelan ko maan bethe...
Ki sacha pyar adhura rehta hai...aur aap usi huq se...
Wo humpe pal do pal ki mohabbat ka ehsaan kar bethe...*

Chitra Nandola

Kehte the puri zindagi saath jiyenge...
Aur pal do pal mein hi saath kho bethe...
Aur aap...
Wo hum pe pal do pal ki mohabbat ka ehsaan kar baithe...

Shukra khuda ka iss naachiz ki zindagi mein pyaar kya hota hai ye jatane
ke liye...
Aur isi vaste aap...
Wo hum pe pal do pal ki mohabbat ka ehsaan kar baithe..."
-Itra

Chitra Nandola

A warm note!

I respect and love all of you who read my book. I'm obliged and want blessing and support from you. If you are a young reader and if you have ever hurt someone like this, you must say sorry to that person. And I'm damn sure that, that person will forgive you. Spread love and happiness in the world around you. Nothing is definite in this world. No one knows where destiny will take them. But be kind and do good to those who really care about you and love you. If my book will help even one person then my efforts in writing this book will be successful. And I'll be glad to hear your story from you. If you feel like sharing your story and want to give me this opportunity of publishing your story then it will be a huge privilege for me.

With lots and lots of love
Chitra Nandola

Chitra Nandola